Raspberry Choco
Dolphin Bay Coz
Book 1

By Leena Clover

Chapter 1

Anna Butler stomped her foot and muttered a string of oaths, shaking her head in disbelief. Was it really happening?

She stared at the paper she held in her hand, the one she had eagerly pulled out of the official brown envelope she had ripped open. Her future depended on the contents of that letter. A future she felt she had earned after the trials of the past two years. But apparently, her life would never be a bed of roses.

The powers that be had just rejected her application. That meant she would not be opening her dream café any time soon. Bayside Books, the bookstore she had lovingly tended for the past twenty years would remain just that. There would be no aroma of freshly brewed coffee mingling with the musty old books. And there would be no happy customers licking the frosting off her delicious cupcakes.

In a daze, Anna turned off the stand mixer beating a gallon of butter cream frosting and stared at the mess around her. The massive granite island in her updated kitchen was covered in a fine dusting of flour. Packets of melting butter lay next to giant mixing bowls. Tiny jars of spices stood open next to a canister of powdered sugar. A dozen freshly baked cupcakes rested on a cake stand, ready to be frosted.

Anna felt her knees wobble as she pulled herself up on a bar stool. She had barely gulped down half a cup of oatmeal that morning, eager to get on with her baking. Her heart had raced as she eagerly waited for the mail to arrive. A little bird at the town hall had told her a letter had been dispatched to her. Unfortunately, it wasn't what Anna expected.

Anna had lived in the quaint seaside town of Dolphin Bay all her life. She went to college at the local university and married as soon as she got her degree. Thirty four years of wedded bliss had ended abruptly when her husband John met an unexpected demise. Anna had been fifty five, just old enough to dream about retirement, too young to be a widow. She stumbled through the next year, leading a rudderless existence. But her troubles weren't over. A nagging pain below her armpit turned out to be breast cancer.

Anna found herself thrust down a new rabbit hole. The past year had been relentless, consumed by endless visits to specialists and hospitals. There had been a brief period of uncertainty when Anna thought she was on her way to meet John, but the tide had turned in her favor. It had been a month since her last radiation treatment and Anna was recovering well. But she had promised herself she would stop taking things for granted. She would stop putting things off. She had almost tasted death. She had a lot to do before she actually met it.

Anna's eyes flickered as she gazed out of the kitchen windows. Turquoise blue water shimmered in the California sun. A trio of cabanas lay by the poolside, each shaded by a giant umbrella. A tanned, curvy body occupied one of the chairs, dressed in a bikini that could not be called modest in any universe. Anna sighed at the thought of her grown daughter wasting another day lounging by the pool. Then she decided to let it go. She needed to pick her battles.

The kitchen door was flung open as a large red headed woman barged in. Her excess weight agreed with her, giving her a larger than life personality that consumed everything around her.

"What's with all this mess, Anna?" Julie Walsh demanded, looking around with her hands on her hips.

Anna stared blankly as Julie's eyebrows bunched together and her sapphire blue eyes flashed with impatience.

"Did you forget about our lunch date?" Julie asked sharply. "How could you, Anna? I stopped mid-way through a chapter to get ready and come over."

Julie Walsh was a romance author of some repute. She was always on a deadline, scrambling to get things done before the next release. Julie barely spared a minute for most people. But she never missed weekly lunch with her friends Anna and Mary.

Anna picked up the offensive letter and handed it to Julie.

"There must be some mistake," Julie said, staring at the brief communication. "You are not going to take this lying down, are you?"

Anna suddenly felt the weight of the past year on her shoulders.

"What can I do?" she asked meekly. "They have already made their decision."

"Not worth the paper it's written on," Julie blustered. "Get off your keister, Anna Butler! We are taking care of this right now."

"Is something wrong?" a soft voice asked.

Anna turned around to welcome her friend Mary. Mary was the exact opposite of Julie, and older than both women. Her green eyes were filled with trepidation as she stared at her friends.

"You are not sick again, are you, Anna?"

"I am not ill, Mary," Anna assured her.

"Take a look at this," Julie ordered, thrusting the paper in Mary's face. "We all know who's behind this."

"We do?" Anna asked, looking puzzled.

"This has Lara Crawford written all over it," Julie said sternly. "Surely you recognize that, Anna?"

Lara Crawford was the mayor of Dolphin Bay. The whole town knew she had it in for Anna Butler. Anna had learned to ignore the brash woman. It seemed to anger her even more and Anna bore the brunt of it in many different ways.

"Why would Lara be involved in this?" Anna asked.

Julie banged a fist on the kitchen island, upsetting a box of baking soda.

"She knows how much the café means to you. She will do anything to make sure you don't succeed."

Mary nodded in agreement.

"You know I don't like to malign anyone. But I agree with Julie. Lara Crawford is pure evil. You need to fight this, Anna."

Mary and Julie pulled Anna off the stool and made her fix her face. A fresh coat of lipstick later, the three women marched to the town hall, ready to beard the lioness in her den.

A mousy, bespectacled young girl outside the mayor's office tried in vain to thwart them.

"Step aside," Julie warned. "Lara's expecting us."

Anna had shrugged off her gloom on the way and summoned all her inner strength. She barged in on Julie's heels and sat down before the odious woman who was trying to steal her dream.

Lara Crawford's mouth was set in a sneer. Her crooked nose did nothing to soften her appearance. Nor did her power suit or the strand of expensive pearls she wore around her neck.

"Is it my lucky day?" she crooned. "Dolphin Bay's famous husband killer is here to see me."

"Stop that nonsense," Julie snapped. She turned to Anna and tipped her head. "Go on, Anna."

Anna placed the letter she had received before Lara.

"Why was my application rejected?"

Lara rolled her eyes.

"Vendor licensing is not in my purview."

"This is your signature, Lara," Anna pointed out. "Do you deny that?"

"I sign dozens of documents in a day," Lara drawled. "But I am not always the decision maker."

"You know what Anna has been through, Lara," Mary said softly. "Have a heart."

"You mean how she's roaming scot free after killing her husband?" Lara asked with relish. "I wouldn't know."

"You are crossing the line, Lara," Julie warned. She took Anna's hand in hers and gave it a squeeze. "The police could never establish what happened to John."

"But I know," Lara pounced, flinging a finger at Anna. "She killed him in cold blood."

Anna shrank back in her seat. She was barely keeping it together.

"That's enough," Julie chided. "Stop abusing your power, Lara. Or you won't be sitting in that chair much longer."

"I am going to prove it," Lara hissed. "That's a promise you can take to the bank."

Anna scraped her chair back and stood up.

"I am going to open my café whether you like it or not,

Lara. That's my promise to you."

She walked out with her head high.

"Watch out, Lara," Julie warned and followed her friend out.

"Stop being mean, Lara," Mary said with a soft sigh.

She was the last one to leave the room.

Lara Crawford leaned back in her chair and allowed herself a malicious grin. She had won the battle. She had plenty more tricks up her sleeve to make Anna Butler suffer. She would do anything to succeed in her mission. She planned to drive the Butler women out of Dolphin Bay.

Chapter 2

Cassandra Butler gathered her waist length golden hair and tied it in a knot on the top of her head. Her wet, shapely body carried an extra ten pounds around the middle. The spring sun warmed her back, bare except for a flimsy string bikini. She had taken care to slather it with sunscreen lotion. A healthy tan was one thing, but she couldn't risk ruining her flawless complexion with freckles or sunburn.

Cassie swam a dozen leisurely laps in her mother's swimming pool, reveling in the sense of wellbeing that stole over her. Very few things made her feel content nowadays. Being one with the water was an easy way to let go of all her worries.

Life had dealt Cassie a few hard blows. She was still reeling from the last one. Her crooked manager had absconded with most of her hard earned money, leaving her with a big tax bill. The coveted golden knight otherwise called an Oscar award lay forgotten at the back of her sock drawer. When she won the award at 21, it had been her crowning glory. At 36, it looked like it was going to be her swan song. Cassie wasn't sure if she cared much either way.

She stepped out of the pool and settled into her favorite cabana, letting the sun dry her. Her phone chirped and her face lit up as her best bud's face flashed on the screen.

"It's about time," she said with a pout, activating the video feature on the phone.

A buff, bare-chested man blew a kiss at her and laughed. It was hard to tell he was ten years younger.

"Don't sulk, Cassie. It will give you wrinkles."

Cassie straightened her mouth immediately and smiled. "So when are you getting here, Bobby? I have great plans for us."

Bobby placed a proprietary hand over his six pack abs and winced.

"I don't think I can make it this weekend, sweetie. Fox booked a last minute session for tomorrow."

Bobby was in big demand in Hollywood as a personal trainer to the stars. Making celebrities sweat was his job and he was good at it.

"I thought you had a new Pilates routine for me."

"Why don't you come to La-La land instead?" Bobby asked. "I should be done by midnight tomorrow. We can party all night and go shopping on Rodeo Drive on Sunday. It's not like you have to hurry back."

Cassie's face fell.

"Rodeo Drive's off limits for me, Bobbykins. You know that."

"Don't worry about the money, babe. I'll take care of it."

Cassie felt her cheeks burn with shame. She chatted with her friend for a while, her mind wandering to a time when she could squander a few thousand on an afternoon of casual shopping. She hung up after Bobby promised to visit soon.

Cassie took a long sip of icy lemon water and contemplated her life. She had been doing it for the past several months, ever since she came back home to take care of her ailing mother. The day stretched before her, full of nothing to do. She closed her eyes and placed her arms below her head, poised to take a nap.

A hum of muffled voices woke her. She sat up and peered at the scene playing out in the kitchen. Her mother had been bustling around all morning, baking yet another batch of cupcakes. Now she had been joined by two women. Cassie spotted the large plaid covered body of Julie Walsh, her mother's bossy author friend. The mousy Mary Sullivan stood by meekly, looking like a 1950s housewife in her green floral dress.

Cassie was used to seeing the two women around the house. The Firecrackers as they called themselves had been friends since before her birth. Apparently nothing could come between them. Cassie secretly envied them their bond.

The tableau inside the house unfurled quickly with Julie getting more excited by the minute. She waved her arms around, urging Cassie's mother Anna to do something. Finally, the women seemed to make up their minds. Cassie watched anxiously as they hurried out of the house. She waited to hear a car engine come to life. Surely her mother hadn't decided to walk in the blazing sun? What was she thinking?

Cassie moved with uncharacteristic swiftness and hurried inside. The house appeared dark after the glaring sun but she didn't have time to let her eyes adjust. Cassie walked into her closet and pulled on the first pair of jeans she could lay her hands on. A white tunic followed. Combing her hair with her fingers, Cassie grabbed her Prada bag, tied an Hermes silk scarf around her neck and rushed out to her car.

The ancient Mercedes convertible roared to life after a few attempts. Cassie floored the gas pedal and took off with a screech, trying not to think of the beloved Ferrari she had sold to appease the tax man. She reached the corner of Main Street in five minutes. Pulling into the parking lot that straddled the street, Cassie sat in the car, trying to spot her mother. Cassie had no idea what she would say to her. Anna had made it clear she didn't need to be cosseted, ill or not.

Cassie slouched in her seat and fiddled with the radio to pass the time. A couple of young women walked past with toddlers in tow. People streamed in and out of the local pub, The Tipsy Whale. It was a popular spot for lunch. Cassie debated going in to get a sandwich. She thought back longingly to the organic smoothie bowls her neighborhood café in Beverly Hills was famous for. She hoped her mother would have some healthier dishes on the menu when she opened her café. She thought of the array of cakes Anna had been experimenting with and decided it wasn't likely.

Tired of toasting in the heat, Cassie got out of the car. She walked around Main Street twice, wondering where Anna was. Although her mother was fully capable of taking care of herself, Cassie remembered the oncologist's warning. Anna wasn't supposed to go out in the sun. Her skin was still raw from the radiation and she needed to protect it from more damage.

A babble of familiar voices fell upon her ears. She whirled around and saw the Firecrackers walking out of the town hall building. Anna's head was uncovered and the peasant blouse she wore over her capris laid her shoulders bare. Cassie frowned, angered by her mother's carelessness.

Anna looked quiet and thoughtful as she walked with her friends toward the pub. The three women entered the Tipsy Whale, Julie Walsh looking like she was ready to murder anyone who crossed her path.

Cassie's stomach growled and she came to a quick decision. She strode toward the pub. Her mouth watered as she thought of what she would order for lunch. Murphy, the pub owner, was famous up and down the coast for his humungous sandwiches.

Julie Walsh stood in line at the bar, waiting to order. Cassie looked around furtively and spotted her mother sitting at a window table with her friend Mary. Julie boomed a greeting when she saw her, insisting Cassie join them for lunch.

"Some other time," Cassie said smoothly. "I am expecting a call from my agent."

"Well, in that case …" Julie hesitated. "I won't keep you."

Cassie put in an order for the roast turkey on sourdough. It came with hickory smoked bacon and avocado and loads of local Monterey Jack cheese. Cassie tried to add up the calories she was about to consume, thinking of the fat grams and carbs that were taboo to her peers. Then she gave up. She would have plenty of time to shed some weight after she landed a good role. Cassie eagerly accepted her sandwich from an apron clad girl, sniffing hungrily at the delicious smells wafting through it. She turned around swiftly and landed into a solid wall.

"Hello Princess," a deep, throaty voice whispered in her ear.

Cassie felt her knee pop as she looked into a pair of brown eyes the color of creamy milk chocolate. She was a bit too familiar with who they belonged to.

"Dylan," she said in a clipped voice. "What are you doing here?"

"Getting a bite to eat," the tall, tanned man answered, rubbing his nose. "Same as you."

Cassie nodded and walked to her mother's table. Anna and her friends were devouring their lunch with relish.

"Can I give you a ride?" Cassie asked the women.

"We can walk back," Anna said primly. "Your car's too small for all of us."

Julie struck her down. "Don't be silly, Anna. We can squeeze in." She nodded at Cassie. "We are almost done here."

"I'll be waiting in the car," Cassie said. "No need to rush."

She pulled off her scarf and handed it to her mother, ignoring the stubborn expression that settled on her face. Cassie bent down and wound the scarf around her mother's neck, showing her she meant business.

She walked out of the pub without a backward glance, ready to take a hefty bite out of her sandwich.

Chapter 3

Anna rose with the sun. She walked into her kitchen and poured herself a cup of coffee. Her husband John had talked her into buying the new fangled coffee maker his last Christmas. He barely got time to enjoy it.

Anna knew Cassie wouldn't be up for hours yet. She clucked in disapproval and headed out to the patio. Anna was meticulous about her daily yoga routine. It centered her and got her ready for the day.

Cassie was sitting at the kitchen counter when Anna went back in.

"You're up early."

Cassie shrugged and added a generous amount of cream to her coffee.

"Are we out of cereal?" she grumbled.

Anna pulled out a box of 7 grain cereal from the pantry.

"Not those sticks!" Cassie complained. "They taste like dust. Where are my frosted flakes?"

"I threw them out," Anna said lightly. "All that sugar is not good for you."

"Says the woman who bakes cupcakes by the dozen,"

Cassie said with a roll of her eyes.

"I use raw sugar or natural sweeteners," Anna snapped. "Not the same as processed food."

Cassie sulked. She drained her coffee and jumped down from her perch, ready to head to her room. Anna had a flashback to a similar moment twenty years ago. Had her daughter changed even a little in the past two decades?

"Why don't I fix you some breakfast?" she cajoled. "Some oatmeal will go down nicely."

"Oatmeal? Yuck! You know I hate oatmeal, Mom!"

"I thought you film types ate healthy stuff. Oatmeal is healthy."

"Maybe," Cassie said. "Doesn't mean I have to like it."

"How about avocado toast then?" Anna asked. "With a poached egg on top?"

Cassie brightened.

"That sounds cool."

Fifteen minutes later, Anna dished up the tasty breakfast.

"Bobby will have a fit if he sees me eating this," Cassie said, taking a big bite of her toast.

Anna let out a snort. Bobby had come up with an age appropriate diet plan for Anna. It hadn't gone down well.

"What's your plan for the day?" she asked. "Why don't you come to the bookstore later?"

"I'm busy, Mom."

"Doing what? Lying by the pool?" Anna spoke sharply. "You are too young to fritter your life away."

"It's my life. Let me decide what to do with it."

Anna bit back a retort. She didn't want to start the day with yet another fight with her daughter.

"I'll be at the store if you need me."

"What am I, 12?" Cassie wiped her plate clean with the last piece of toast. She picked up her coffee and went out to the pool.

Anna cleared up and went into her bedroom to fix herself. She observed herself in the full length mirror. Her clothes hung loose on her short frame, making her look gaunt. She ran a quick brush through her pixie cut salt and pepper hair. It had taken a while to grow back after her treatment. She was just getting used to the short style. The grey was new. Anna wondered if it made her look older.

A light mist was clearing up when Anna stepped out of her door. She climbed her trusty bicycle and pedaled out, admiring the wisteria that bloomed over her front porch.

Anna's store Bayside Books was situated at the corner of Main Street and Ocean Avenue. It had large windows that looked out over the Coastal Walk and some rocky bluffs. The dark blue waters of the bay shimmered in the distance.

Anna rested her bike against the wall of her store and looked up at the giant magnolia tree that stood guard over the entrance. The pink and white buds were just beginning to bloom. Anna breathed in the fresh lemony scent of the flowers and went inside. She immediately found her lips stretching into a smile.

Bayside Books was a haven for all book lovers. Floor to ceiling bookshelves covered every wall, overflowing with volumes. Every available surface had a stack of books on it. Plush armchairs were strewn across the space, inviting readers to settle down and browse through their favorite book at their leisure. Reading tables were placed by the windows, providing a priceless view of the cliffs and the water.

Anna went into a small pantry tucked behind her desk. It was just big enough to hold a refrigerator and a tiny sink with barely enough counter space for a coffee machine. Anna plugged in the coffee, picked up a feather duster and started the tedious chore of dusting all the bookshelves. It was the first thing she did after she came to the store every day.

Anna fretted over the fate of her café. She had dreamed about it with her husband John. They had meticulously saved for the expansion. Maybe it was destined to be just a pipe dream.

The phone rang, snapping Anna out of her reverie. It was her old friend Vicki Bauer. They hadn't talked in years, not since John passed. Vicki had sent flowers for the funeral but she hadn't made it to the memorial service. Most people in town hadn't, thanks to the vicious rumors Lara

Crawford had started. Anna remembered feeling abandoned by Vicki at that time.

"Vicki! It's good to hear the sound of your voice. It's been a while."

Vicki reciprocated by saying something similar.

"How are things?" Anna asked, meaning to get to the purpose of the call right away. "All well?"

"Everything is fine," Vicki assured her. "Oh Anna … I was thinking … do you remember Book Club? Didn't we have the best time with it?"

"I do remember," Anna said coldly. "We still have a Book Club in Dolphin Bay. It meets here in the bookshop every Wednesday."

Vicki cleared her throat.

"I've been meaning to come to that," she wheedled, "But you know how it is with kids. Life's a bit overwhelming right now."

"We all feel it, dear."

"I was thinking about the other book club, the Crime Solvers' Club."

"Oh!" Anna dismissed. "That was just a bit of fun, Vicki."

"Not entirely," Vicki reminded her. "We managed to solve a mystery or two."

"If you say so," Anna said moodily.

She was still not sure what Vicki wanted from her.

"Why did it fizzle out?" Vicki asked.

"Why the sudden interest in the past, Vicki?" Anna asked. "What's bothering you?"

Vicki broke down. Anna could hear her sobbing on the phone.

"Everything is not fine, Anna," she said through her tears. "I need your help."

"Go on."

"It's my son, Cody."

"I remember Cody," Anna nodded. "He must be what, 19, 20 by now? Is he in college?"

"He's a senior at Dolphin Bay University," Vicki said, her voice filling up with pride. "He's doing good there. Or he was …"

Anna waited patiently while Vicki indulged in another round of sobbing.

"Get a hold of yourself, Vicki," she ordered. "Get to the point."

"A girl from the college was found dead. The police think my Cody killed her."

"What?"

Anna sat down in her chair. Vicki had her undivided attention now.

"Cody barely knew her. The police took him in for questioning. They are saying he is their top suspect. What am I going to do, Anna?"

"You need to get him a lawyer," Anna told her.

"I'm working on that," Vicki said. "But I need someone who can help clear my boy of blame."

"What can I do?" Anna asked.

"You are good at solving mysteries," Vicki said. "I want you to get to the bottom of this."

"Crime Solvers' Club was just for fun," Anna argued. "Your boy's life is at stake here, Vicki. Maybe you should hire a professional investigator."

"At least come and meet Cody," Vicki pleaded. "He's in shock. He won't say anything. But he might talk to you. You were his favorite out of all my friends."

"Let me think about it," Anna said grudgingly.

She hung up after promising to get in touch with Vicki soon. The next thing she did was call the Firecrackers. She didn't make big decisions without consulting them.

Julie answered her phone immediately.

"Let me patch Mary in," she said.

Anna didn't waste time in bringing them up to speed.

"Lara's already making trouble for you, Anna," Mary said quietly. "Are you sure you want to butt horns with the police?"

"I know how it feels to be condemned without trial," Anna told them. "This poor kid has his whole life ahead of him."

"What if he is guilty?" Julie cut in.

"Then I'll be the first to turn him in," Anna said resolutely.

The three friends agreed to meet at Julie's before heading out to meet Vicki and her son.

Anna hung up and called Cassie.

"What is it, Mom?" Cassie's irritation traveled along the phone line.

Anna imagined her reclining in her favorite cabana by the pool.

"I need you to come watch the store, dear."

"I'm expecting a call from my agent."

"You can take the call here," Anna shot back. "Please get here soon, Cassie. I have to leave in fifteen minutes."

Anna smiled, feeling thankful for small mercies. At least Cassie would get out of the house now.

Chapter 4

Cassie lay in her favorite cabana, trying to catch some warmth from the watery sunlight. Her mother had left for the bookstore and wouldn't be back before evening.

Cassie stood up, yawned and stepped into the pool. She had given up her rigorous exercise regimen since coming back to Dolphin Bay. But she still swam twenty laps every day, regardless of the season.

She placed a call to Bobby. He sent her a text message saying he was in the middle of a training session.

The phone rang. Cassie frowned when her mother's name flashed on the screen.

"What is it, Mom?"

Anna wanted her to go and mind the store. Cassie protested for a while before giving in. Bayside Books was new to Cassie. The store had been closed for most of the time Cassie had been back home so she didn't really know her way around it.

Cassie dragged her feet getting ready. She pulled on a black shirt over faded jeans, wrapped a silk scarf around her neck, slapped her shades on and she was done. A spritz of Joy perfume and some red lipstick made her feel human. The little Mercedes spun its tires and Cassie was walking into the store five minutes later.

"Where are you off to?" she asked her mother. "Don't forget your hat."

"Stop nagging me," Anna grumbled. "I'm just going to Julie's."

"Now?" It was Cassie's turn to complain. "I thought there was some crisis here."

"There is," Anna said curtly. "We can talk about it later."

Anna gave Cassie specific instructions about how to handle the customers. Cassie nodded her head absent mindedly, busy admiring the view from the windows.

"I got it, Mom. It's not rocket science."

"You were always a quick learner."

Anna leaned forward impulsively to hug her daughter. Cassie took a step back involuntarily. Anna's face fell.

"See you later," she said, summoning some false cheer and stepped out.

Cassie bit her tongue and berated herself as she saw her mother ride her bike away from the store.

Cassie walked around the store, looking at the overflowing shelves. She tilted her head to read the titles off the spines and found herself smiling. She had been a voracious reader as a child. But she didn't have the time once she started working. The only thing she had read plenty of in the past twenty years were scripts. Scripts and society magazines.

A young girl walked into the store with her father. She wanted to look at the Harry Potter books. There was a steady stream of people coming in after that and Cassie stayed busy helping them. Some of them seemed like regulars. They walked confidently to a shelf, pulled out a book and settled down in an armchair without a word to Cassie. Cassie decided her mother was being too lenient with the locals. No wonder the store was bleeding money.

Cassie was watching a cat video Bobby sent her when she heard the two women. She hadn't seen them come in. Cassie figured they were housewives in their late twenties. They were weighed down by bags from the local grocery store. A baguette was thrust into one while the other overflowed with asparagus stocks.

"I thought the redwood forest was safe," the woman with a shock of blonde curls gushed. "We go for a hike there every Sunday."

"No such thing as a safe place nowadays," the other said dourly.

She wore a dress a couple of sizes too large. Cassie figured she had either lost a lot of weight suddenly or she bought her clothes at the thrift store.

"But what was she doing there alone?"

"Obviously she wasn't alone," Dour Face scoffed. "There was at least one person ..."

The blonde haired woman gasped.

"Oh, you mean ..."

Cassie cleared her throat.

"What are you girls talking about?"

"Haven't you heard?" Both women chorused.

"It's front page news in the Dolphin Bay Chronicle, of course," the blonde headed woman forged ahead. "Anna gets the paper."

She walked to the reading table by the window and picked up a stack of newspapers.

"I'm sure you will tell it better," Cassie coaxed.

"They found a girl dead in the woods," the dour faced woman said in a hushed voice. "Rumor is she was murdered."

"No way!" Cassie exclaimed. "In this sleepy town? Nothing ever happens here."

"It does now," the blonde haired woman said bluntly. "The police already have the killer pegged down. They should be making an arrest soon."

"How do you know that?" Cassie wondered.

"Haven't you been out and about? Everyone's talking about it."

Dour Face was looking at Cassie oddly.

"Have I seen you somewhere?" she asked. "You look familiar."

Cassie assured her there was no chance of that.

"I know," the blonde haired woman exclaimed.

The other woman had been calling her Taffy or Daffy. Cassie wasn't really sure which.

"She looks like that woman who works at the car dealership out on the highway," Taffy said.

"The one who's always blowing her nose?"

"That's the one," Taffy said triumphantly. "She has a really long nose and a mustache."

The women giggled and whispered loud enough for everyone to hear. Cassie took deep breaths and counted to what felt like hundred.

The two women finally left.

Cassie picked up the newspaper and skimmed through the front page article. It was surprisingly well written although it was light on the details.

Cassie's stomach rumbled. The clock on the wall showed it was after 2 PM. No wonder she was feeling light headed. She debated leaving the store for a few minutes to go grab something to eat. Did her mother do that?

Cassie went into the pantry, hoping to find a snack in the refrigerator. She found a bunch of takeout menus on a shelf. She ordered the sandwich of the day from the Tipsy Whale. Murphy took her order but warned her it would take a while. Cassie found a pot of strawberry yogurt in the refrigerator. It wasn't her usual probiotic organic brand. Then Cassie remembered it had cost five dollars for an eight ounce container. She couldn't afford it any longer.

A bell dinged somewhere. Cassie walked out, licking the last spoonful of the surprisingly delicious yogurt. She stopped short at the sight of the imposing woman who stood tapping a bell impatiently. Her pink suit proclaimed she dressed according to season. Cassie admired the strand of pearls she wore. She should have got one of those for her mother while she still had money.

"Stop making that racket," she said. "I'm here now."

"Like mother, like daughter," the woman muttered.

"How can I help you?" Cassie asked.

"I'm here to talk about the murder case. Where's Anna?"

"My mother went out," Cassie informed her. She pointed at the front page article in the Chronicle. "Is that what you want to talk about?"

The woman snorted.

"You don't have a clue, do you?"

"About what?" Cassie folded her hands and tried not to stare at the woman's crooked nose. "I am sorry, but have we met before?"

"You don't know who I am?" the woman in the pink suit roared. "How long have you been back in town?"

"Six months," Cassie said. "I've been busy."

"I am Lara Crawford."

"Should that mean something to me?"

"I am the mayor of this town, you ignoramus!"

"Okay, Madam Mayor. Can I take a message for you?"

"Tell Anna it won't be long now. The police will be arresting her soon."

"What are you talking about?" Cassie asked, puzzled.

"You poor girl! Anna killed your father. You are living with a cold blooded murderer."

Cassie's eyes bulged. She couldn't have shown this kind of emotion after a dozen rehearsals.

"I won't let her get away with it," Lara warned and stormed out of the store.

Cassie barely tasted the sandwich the Tipsy Whale delivered. It was barbecued chicken with crunchy slaw, another of their masterpieces.

Anna came back, looking upset. Cassie sprang up, eager to get a load off her chest.

"A mad woman came in here, saying you killed Dad."

"Lara Crawford? She's a nuisance. Just ignore her."

"But this is slander," Cassie cried. "Why are you letting her get away with it?"

Anna spied the discarded sandwich wrapper next to the cash register.

"Didn't I teach you to pick up after yourself?" she asked Cassie.

Cassie defended herself.

"I just finished eating. I was ringing up a purchase."

"Stop making excuses, girl. You are spoilt and that's a fact."

"Maybe I am used to a better life, Mom," Cassie said stubbornly. "My housekeeper took care of this kind of stuff."

Anna rolled her eyes.

"As you can see, there is no fancy maid here. You have to pull your own weight."

Cassie picked up her shades and slammed them on her face.

"Why are you so mean, huh?"

She strode out of the store, simmering with anger. Maybe she wasn't meant to get along with her mother.

Chapter 5

Anna bustled about in her kitchen later that evening, getting dinner ready. She was making Chicken Parmesan as a peace offering for her daughter. Maybe she had been a bit harsh with her. Chicken Parm was Cassie's favorite meal growing up. Anna hoped it would put the smile back on her daughter's face.

She stirred the sauce and slid the crispy chicken into the oven. It was smothered in mozzarella cheese, just the way Cassie liked it.

Cassie came in and peeked at the pot on the stove.

"Smells awesome, Mom," she said. "I missed your cooking."

Anna had been on a hiatus from the kitchen while she was undergoing her treatment. Cassie had insisted on that. She had put together simple meals for them through Anna's surgery and subsequent recovery.

"I am glad to be back in the kitchen," Anna nodded happily. "Why don't you pour us some wine? I just uncorked a nice Pinot Noir for us."

"Are you sure you can drink wine?" Cassie asked, her voice laced with concern.

"It's fine. I talked to the doctor."

"What if you feel queasy or something?"

"Then I will just stop," Anna assured her.

The oven dinged, indicating it was time to eat. Cassie tossed the salad while Anna dished up the spaghetti. Cassie cut into her chicken eagerly and popped a piece in her mouth. Anna was looking at her, waiting for her reaction.

Cassie moaned in delight.

"It's delicious, Mom. Just like I remember it."

Anna's spine relaxed and she finally took a bite herself.

"I'm sorry I walked out earlier," Cassie said, twirling spaghetti on her fork. "You know I have a short fuse."

"You did have a temper," Anna chuckled. "Even in kindergarten."

They reminisced a bit about Cassie's childhood. Cassie relaxed as they chatted comfortably, sipping the excellent wine.

"What was the crisis earlier, Mom? Did you take care of it?"

Anna brought her up to speed.

"One of my old friends is in trouble. Or her son is. They are saying he murdered a girl."

"Wait a minute," Cassie said. "Is this the girl they found dead in the woods?"

"That's right," Anna nodded. "Vicki's boy Cody is the top suspect. She believes he is innocent though."

"Of course she does," Cassie countered. "She's his mother."

"I am not going to protect the boy if he turns out to be guilty. I'm just after the truth."

"Why are you getting involved? And who is this Vicki? I have never heard of her."

"We used to be in a book club," Anna explained. "It was after you left home."

"I am guessing it was more than a book club," Cassie said shrewdly.

Anna laughed. "You guessed that right. We got pulled into solving a couple of cases. We called ourselves the Crime Solvers, just for fun. Then John passed. I got sick. The whole thing kind of fell apart."

"And she came running back to you, now that she's in trouble? You must be good at this thing, Mom."

Anna shrugged.

The doorbell chimed, interrupting them. Anna scrambled to her feet.

"Are you expecting a package or something?"

Cassie shook her head. She served herself a second helping of the Chicken Parm while Anna went to the front door.

She came back with a tall, hefty man with a thick crop of salt and pepper hair.

Anna introduced them.

"Chief Mancini, meet my daughter Cassandra."

Cassie tried not to stare at the handsome stranger. His cognac eyes crinkled at the corners as he gave her a warm smile.

"I am not the police chief any more, Mrs. Butler. Haven't been for a while. Call me Gino."

"Then you must call me Anna."

Cassie remembered her manners and poured him a glass of wine. Gino Mancini sniffed the glass like a pro and took a small sip.

"Perfetto! 2013 was a good year for us."

"Gino is the owner of Mystic Hill winery," Anna said, nodding at the label on the wine bottle. "This is his wine."

"A policeman who is also a vintner," Cassie mused. "That's a strange combination."

Gino laughed wholeheartedly. Dimples appeared on either side of his mouth, softening his rugged looks.

"My grandpa started Mystic Hill more than fifty years ago. You can say wine runs in my blood. I took some time sowing my wild oats. Had a stint in the Air Force. A spot on the police force opened just when I wanted to come home. Now I am retired from law enforcement. I spend my days tending my grapes and making wine."

"That sounds like an interesting life," Cassie smiled, raising her glass to him.

"How about you?" Gino asked her. "Word around town is you are some kind of actress?"

"Not just any actress," Anna boasted. "My Cassie won an Oscar award when she was 21. She's very talented."

Cassie colored.

"I'm taking a break right now," she said moodily.

"There's an amateur theatre group in town," Gino said. "I am a backstage volunteer. Maybe you can come and give us some pointers?"

"I'll think about it," Cassie promised.

There was an awkward pause and they all pretended to sip the wine.

"I suppose you are here to talk about the murder?" Anna asked.

Gino turned serious.

"I am here to caution you, Anna. Lara Crawford is making a lot of noise. She might just succeed in reopening John's case."

"Where did you hear that?" Anna asked. "Did she come

talk to you?"

"Not yet. But I have my sources at the police department."

"What's spurring her on?" Anna asked, concerned. "Have they found any new evidence?"

"Not to my knowledge."

Cassie was following their conversation eagerly.

"Why is this woman getting involved, Mom? Looks like she's out to get you."

Anna sighed deeply.

"Lara was your father's friend. Somehow, she latched on to this idea that I wanted to harm your father. I don't know why. She knew how much I loved him."

"You never told me about this," Cassie said, pursing her lips in disapproval.

"I didn't think it was something I could talk about over the phone," Anna explained. "I was planning to tell you at the funeral."

Cassie had never made it to her father's funeral. She had been stuck in Mexico, filming for her telenovela.

"The whole town rose against your mother at that time," Gino spoke up. "Many people didn't come for the funeral. She got the silent treatment everywhere she went, thanks to Lara Crawford and the rumors she spread."

"I didn't know any of this," Cassie said soberly. "It must have been hard on you, Mom."

"It was unexpected," Anna agreed. "Your father did so much for the needy. He deserved a good farewell."

Her eyes teared up as she thought of her husband.

"That's why I want to help Cody," Anna said with resolve. "I know how gossip can ruin a person's reputation."

"Poor kid," Gino clucked. "Did he even know that girl?"

"Apparently, they were madly in love. He wanted to ask her to marry him."

"How do you know that?" Gino asked.

"I know his mother," Anna explained. "She thinks I can find the real killer. But I barely know where to start."

"Shouldn't be hard for you," Gino said with a twinkle in his eye. "You have done this before."

"That was a long time ago," Anna said morosely. "I may have to pick your brain on this, Gino."

"You are welcome anytime. But I need to scrape some rust off my brain."

"Don't be so modest. You were the best police chief this town has had in recent history. Not sure your successor is that competent."

"I can't comment on that," Gino said slyly. "Looks like you

have your plate full, Anna. Beware of Lara though. I think you should talk to your lawyer about this."

"You don't think I am guilty?" she asked him. She turned toward her daughter. "What about you, Cassie? Do you think I am capable of murdering your father?"

"Of course not," Cassie shot back loyally. "I think this woman is misusing her power. She's just being catty."

"Whatever her motivation, you will have to deal with her," Gino warned.

Anna's special meal had grown cold while they talked.

"Can I offer you some dessert?" she asked Gino. "Tiramisu. Cassie's favorite. It's my Nona's recipe."

"I didn't know you were Italian," Gino remarked.

"My mother was Italian, so I guess I'm half Italian. My grandparents came to America at the turn of the last century."

"So we have a common heritage," Gino smiled.

Anna fought a blush. She turned around to pull a pan of tiramisu from the refrigerator. Gino didn't object to the generous helping she dished out.

"You ought to open a café or something," he said, smacking his lips.

Anna thought of her rejected café license and resolved to fight for her dream.

Chapter 6

Anna Butler sat out on her patio the next morning, savoring her first cup of coffee. A riot of daffodils bloomed in a corner, their bright yellow hue making her feel optimistic about the day ahead.

She had been up early to bake a fresh batch of her raspberry chocolate cupcakes. They were cooling on a rack in her kitchen, ready to be frosted.

Gino Mancini had compelled her to think seriously about what lay around the corner. But she was determined to put her own troubles aside and make some headway in learning more about Cody Bauer's girlfriend, the young victim.

Anna went back in and started cutting avocadoes for breakfast. Her own avocado tree had died of neglect but the local farm produced a good crop. Anna squeezed a lemon over the avocado slices to keep them from going brown and mashed them up. She was sprinkling hot sauce over her toast when Cassie walked in, sleepy eyed.

Anna got a mumbled greeting before Cassie slumped into a chair and poured herself some coffee. She sipped it with her eyes half closed.

"What are you doing today?" Anna asked her, nudging a plate of avocado toast in her direction.

Cassie yawned widely.

"I don't know, Mom. My agent might call about a new role."

"That's what you said yesterday."

"So?" Cassie shrugged, draining her coffee and frowning at the empty pot.

"You need to make a fresh pot," Anna told her. "I will be at the store. There are plenty of leftovers for your lunch."

Cassie grunted and slouched in her chair, closing her eyes again.

Anna wished her daughter would take an interest in something. She went to her room and called Julie.

"We need to come up with a plan of action," she told her. "How's your calendar looking today?"

"I'm between chapters," Julie said. "I can spare a couple of hours. Shall we meet at the store?"

"Let me call Mary," Anna said.

Mary had been waiting for their call. They generally chatted in the morning to talk about their day's plans.

Julie and Mary needed half an hour to get ready. Anna dressed in a bright yellow top inspired by the daffodils and slapped a straw hat on her head. She cycled to Bayside Books, thinking about what she wanted to discuss with her friends. She decided not to mention Gino Mancini's visit.

Anna placed her bike in its usual spot and took a moment

to admire Main Street. Brick fronts and striped awnings gave it a picturesque, vintage look. Oak trees lined the street on both sides, casting some welcome shade on the sidewalks. The ancient clock tower stood at the other end, next to the town hall. There was a steady stream of early shoppers visiting the grocery store. The florist was setting out pots of fresh flowers. Anna waved at a couple of people before going into her own store.

She had dusted all the shelves and made coffee by the time Julie breezed in. Julie eyed the plate of cupcakes resting on a table and made a beeline for it.

"Mmmm ..." she moaned after taking a big bite. "Did you bake these today?"

Anna nodded. "I am still tweaking the recipe."

Mary came in, looking flushed.

"Sorry I am late," she apologized. "I was talking to my lodger."

"It sounds so quaint when you say that," Julie laughed. "Are you renting out rooms again?"

"Just the bedroom over the garage," Mary explained. "We have more than enough space with the kids gone. A little extra income doesn't hurt."

"I hear ya," Anna harrumphed.

"I wouldn't feel safe doing it," Julie said, embarking on her pet theme. "What do you know about these people, anyway? Do you even look at their IDs?"

"Rain's a slip of a girl," Mary laughed. "She's not going to hurt us."

"Rain?" Julie rolled her eyes. "I rest my case."

"You'll never guess what happened," Mary continued, ignoring Julie. "Someone almost ran her down the other day."

"And that's why we don't allow cars on Main Street," Anna said with a flourish.

"Come and try these cupcakes, Mary," Julie said. "They are so rich they just melt in your mouth."

"Stop thinking about food for a while, Julie," Mary admonished. "Did you girls read the Chronicle this morning?"

"Not yet," Anna said.

She picked up the local newspaper from the reading table and skimmed the front page. The local murder had once again made headlines.

"Anything worth knowing?" she asked Mary, trying to glean any pertinent information from the paper at the same time.

"The girl's name was Briana. She was a student at the university."

"I knew that but I didn't know her name. Funny that neither Vicki nor Cody mentioned it."

"What else does the paper say?" Julie asked, dabbing her

lips with a tissue.

"Her family moved here recently," Mary continued. "No one seems to know much about them."

"Does that mean she lived at home?" Anna asked.

"I guess so," Mary shrugged. "The paper doesn't say anything about that."

"What difference would that make?" Julie asked.

"I don't know that yet," Anna told them. "I just wondered if she lived in a dorm on campus."

"Does Cody live on campus?" Julie asked.

"You know what? I don't know that. I'll ask him the next time I see him."

"You do that," Julie nodded. "Meanwhile, I can talk to a few people, starting with our mailman. He might tell us something interesting about Briana's family."

"That Alfie is a big gossip," Mary fussed. "And you are no better."

Old Alfie had been the Dolphin Bay mailman since as far back as the girls could remember. He showed no signs of slowing down.

"Alfie and I have an arrangement," Julie grinned. "He keeps me informed with what's happening in town and I keep him supplied with advanced copies of all my books."

"Who would've thought Old Alfie would secretly read romance books?" Anna cackled.

"He's one of my most helpful beta readers," Julie said, defending him.

"What's Cassie doing today?" Mary asked.

Anna shook her head.

"I don't know what to do with that girl."

"She's a grown woman, Anna," Julie consoled. "She's been through a lot. Give her some time to get her bearings."

"Living here must be hard on her," Mary said. "Dolphin Bay might be charming to us, but it pales before the bright lights of Hollywood."

"I didn't ask her to come here," Anna grumbled. "She should have stayed away, like she did for the past twenty years."

Julie looked frustrated.

"Anna Butler, you need to count your blessings. You have a daughter who dropped everything to come and nurse you. Cassie loves you so much. Can't you see that?"

"She didn't have much of a choice," Anna said. "That crooked manager of hers took her to the cleaners."

"She's here now," Mary said firmly. "I think she will stick around."

"She'll be gone as soon as she lands a new role," Anna said with certainty.

"So that's what's bothering you?" Julie eyed the last cupcake on the plate. "You don't want to get used to having her around."

Anna's eyes glistened.

"I'm already used to her."

"We don't have to worry about this now," Mary said hurriedly.

"Yes," Julie agreed. "We need to talk about the café, Anna. What are you going to do now?"

"I can't proceed without a license," Anna sighed. "Frankly, I'm stumped. Lara is going to have her way this time."

"We won't let her," Julie said, biting her lip. "We need to rally the troops."

"That's a great idea, Julie," Mary agreed. "What if we come up with a petition? We can collect signatures in favor of the café. Lara will have to bow down to public demand."

"Most people don't even make eye contact with me," Anna complained. "Lara's seen to that."

"I agree some of Lara's cronies give you the cold shoulder," Julie said thoughtfully. "But they are insignificant. Most businesses on Main Street and Ocean Avenue will side with you. You'll see."

49

"We need to plan this well," Mary told them. "This has to be a community event. Something that involves everyone, you know."

"You already thought of something, haven't you?" Julie asked shrewdly. "Come on, Mary. Out with it."

Mary blushed. She didn't like to be the center of attention.

Anna was looking at her with a hopeful expression.

"Well, we could have a potluck."

"What!" Julie guffawed. "You want to make more work for people."

"Let her speak," Anna admonished, holding up a hand. "Go on, Mary."

"Most people have a favorite dish or two they like to show off," Mary explained. "I know I do. We can fire up the grill outside."

"Anna can bake her cupcakes," Julie said thoughtfully. "And we can convince people to vote for the café over hot dogs and potato salad."

"Something like that," Mary said meekly.

Anna finally smiled.

"I think that's an excellent idea. At the very least, we can all have a good time."

"People will stand by you, Anna," Julie stressed. "I am sure of that."

Mary left to run some errands and Julie headed home. A couple of customers trickled in and Anna got busy taking care of them. She went into the pantry to make some fresh coffee and remembered Gino's advice.

Anna placed a call to her lawyer.

"But can they really reopen the case?" she asked worriedly. "What does that mean for me?"

The lawyer wanted to know if they had found any new evidence. Anna wasn't sure about that. The lawyer promised to talk to the local Dolphin Bay authorities and find out more. He would be on hand if Anna needed anything.

Anna didn't feel reassured. She just hoped the police would believe she was innocent.

Chapter 7

Anna walked to the Yellow Tulip diner. It was situated on Ocean Avenue, parallel to Main Street. Ocean and Main made a two mile stretch known as the Downtown Loop. No vehicles were allowed in this area. People either walked or cycled, and kids whizzed around on skateboards.

Anna had asked Cody Bauer to meet her for lunch. She thought he might not be very forthcoming in his mother's presence so she had convinced Vicki to let her meet him alone.

Cody greeted her with a warm hug. Anna beamed up at him. He had grown up to be a fine young man, his athletic build and cornflower blue eyes guaranteed to make the girls swoon.

"How are you, Mrs. Butler?" Cody asked.

"I'm doing good, Cody. But looks like you are not."

Cody's shoulders slumped. Anna urged him into the diner and chose a booth at the other end. She ordered cheeseburgers for the both of them. The diner had a limited menu but they made a mean burger.

Cody picked at his food, refusing to look up. Anna dipped a French fry into ketchup and chewed on it.

"No use moping, my boy," she said. "We both know why

we are here."

"You believe in me, don't you Mrs. Butler?" Cody pleaded. "I would never hurt Briana. I loved her."

"It doesn't matter what I believe," Anna said dryly. "The police must have something incriminating against you."

Cody's eyes flickered and he looked away.

"My mother said you are going to help us get out of this mess."

"I am going to try," Anna nodded. "But you will have to be completely honest with me, Cody. Don't leave anything out, especially the minor details."

Cody finally took a bite of his burger and sighed.

"What do you want to know?"

"I didn't know you attended the local university. Didn't you have a fancy baseball scholarship to some college out east?"

"That fizzled out when I hurt my elbow," he told her. "There was no question of a sports scholarship after that. We couldn't afford out of state tuition so I enrolled into our local college. It's not bad."

"No, it's not," Anna agreed. "My John worked there most of his life. We had a good life."

"People still mention Professor Butler," Cody told her. "He gave a talk at our school once."

"John enjoyed being a mentor," Anna reminisced.

The waitress came over to top up their drinks. Anna got a curious look from her. The grapevine would soon start buzzing with speculation about what Anna was doing having lunch with a suspected murderer.

Anna sipped her soda and stifled a burp.

"How did you meet Briana? She was new in town, wasn't she?"

"Briana didn't grow up here," Cody nodded. "That's how we got together, I guess."

"How do you mean?"

"We ran into each other in the library," Cody explained. "She was a little spitfire. I asked her out for coffee."

"Did you share any classes?"

"She was studying English Lit," Cody said. "I am a business major."

"What happened after you met?"

"Like you said, she was new in town. I offered to show her the sights. It wasn't long before I fell in love with her."

"Did you tell her that?"

"I am sure she knew," Cody blushed.

"How did she feel about it?"

"Briana could be aloof," Cody said thoughtfully. "She didn't want to get involved at first. But she agreed to go on dates. After some time, I figured we were a couple."

"Were you seeing anyone else?" Anna asked cagily.

Cody was indignant.

"Of course not!"

"I don't know what's the latest trend among you Millennials."

"I was going to ask her to marry me," Cody said fervently. "She was the only one for me."

"So you were both what they call exclusive," Anna stressed.

Cody played with the fries on his plate, avoiding looking at Anna.

"Yes. We were exclusive, Mrs. Butler."

Anna exhausted her questions after a while. Cody agreed to get in touch with her if he had any more information to share.

Anna went back to Bayside Books. The afternoon passed slowly. A couple of regulars lounged in chairs, thumbing through their favorite books. They treated the store like a library but Anna didn't mind.

"Will you keep an eye on things, Dolly?" she asked one of the women dozing at the reading table by the window.

The woman nodded, barely opening her eyes.

Anna wheeled her cycle out on the road, trying to figure out if she could make it to the Mystic Hill winery. She debated calling Julie for a ride. But Julie or Mary didn't know about Gino Mancini's visit. In the end, she decided to brave it.

A salty breeze blew in from the bay but the afternoon sun blazed brightly. Anna was out of breath before she exited the Downtown Loop. She stuck to her plan, refusing to admit she wasn't strong enough. Her leg muscles quivered as she pedaled up the small hill leading to Gino's place. A number of frequent stops later, Anna reached the winery, soaked in sweat, her hair plastered to her skull.

She thought about turning back.

Gino spotted her in that instant. He was unloading something from the back of a pickup.

"Anna! What are you doing here? Don't tell me you pedaled up that hill?"

Anna's chest heaved as she tried to answer him.

"Where are my manners!" Gino cried. "You don't need to talk now. Let's get you out of the sun."

Gino led her into the house, a rambling ranch house that seemed far too big for one person. Anna barely had a chance to admire it. It was several degrees cooler inside. Gino led her to a comfortable couch in a sunken living room. He excused himself and went inside, returning a few minutes later with two tall glasses of lemonade.

Anna sipped the cold drink appreciatively, and accepted the tissue Gino handed her.

"I think I was a fool," she admitted. "I shouldn't have attempted the ride here."

"I'm taking you home myself," Gino told her. "No arguments."

"I'm too old and frail to refuse that offer," Anna grumbled. "So I will just say Thank You and accept."

"You don't look old to me," Gino smiled, flashing his dimples. "I bet I have a few years on you."

"I am closer to sixty than fifty," Anna snorted.

"Age is just a number," Gino said softly. He pointed to his heart. "It's what you feel in here that matters."

Anna began to feel human after she finished her lemonade. Gino offered her more.

"I should offer wine but I think you need this more now."

"I spoke to my lawyer today," Anna began, getting around to the purpose of her visit. "He wanted to know if there was any new evidence."

"Not as far as I know. Lara Crawford is implying that we botched up the investigation."

"That's a slur on your record," Anna cried. "What does she have against you?"

"Hard to say," Gino replied. "She's making this her mission. She is really convinced there was foul play."

"What do you think, Gino?"

"Honestly, I stand by what I said two years ago. The evidence was inconclusive. We didn't have enough to seriously suspect anyone. That includes you, Anna."

"What am I going to do now?"

"My advice is to sit tight," Gino said firmly. "Lara Crawford can dig all she wants but she won't find anything. That's because there is nothing to be found."

"I hope it all blows over. I don't want Cassie worrying about it."

"You faced a lot on your own. You must be a strong woman."

Anna blushed.

"I didn't have a choice."

Gino offered her a tour of the place. Anna declined politely.

"I think I will take that ride now. I'm ready to call it a day."

Gino ushered her out to his truck. He placed her bike in the back and opened the door of the cab for her.

"Would you like to come to a wine tasting event?" he asked as he drove into town. "We have one every month. The

Spring event is coming up soon."

"I would love that," Anna smiled. "I already like your wines."

"We are still finalizing the dates," Gino said. "I will get you a flyer when we finish printing them."

"Say Gino," Anna asked as he came to a stop at the drop-off point on Main.

Luckily, it was just across her store and Anna didn't have far to go.

"What kind of evidence do the police have on Cody?"

"I am not plugged into the day to day activities of the police now, Anna," Gino replied. "I left that life far behind."

Anna thanked him for the ride. Gino ignored her protests and walked her to the store, wheeling her bike himself.

"Call me the next time you want to come see me," he told her. "I can come and get you myself."

Anna felt her knees go weak as he held her hands and stared into her eyes, bidding goodbye.

Chapter 8

Cassie lay sprawled on the couch, watching Casablanca. It was her favorite movie of all time. She had worked her way through a big bowl of buttered popcorn. Now she was feasting on potato chips. She ignored the slight nausea she felt from gorging on all the butter and grease.

Humphrey Bogart and Ingrid Bergman talked about Paris on the screen. Cassie was mesmerized. She wondered if she had ever known true love. She had been married twice. Both of her marriages had ended badly. She had suffered some heartbreak when her first husband ditched her for an upcoming starlet. By the time her second husband filed divorce papers, she had become cynical. She had agreed to a mutual divorce, eager to end it all with a minimum of fuss.

Anna came in and collapsed in an armchair. Cassie didn't take her eyes off the screen but she observed her mother from the corner of her eye. She was looking sweaty and exhausted. Cassie wondered what she had been up to.

"This place looks like a trash heap," Anna complained. "How can you make such a mess, Cassie?"

"I'll take care of it later," Cassie said, caught up in the last few scenes of the movie.

"Do it now," Anna ordered, springing to her feet. "What if someone knocked on the door right now?"

"Are you expecting company?" Cassie asked, rooting around in the chip bag for the salty crumbs.

"That's beside the point," Anna said, her voice going up another octave. "This is my living room. It has to be ready for visitors at all times."

Cassie emitted a loud sigh and switched off the TV. She made no move to get up. She leaned further back in her recliner and looked at her mother.

"Why don't you relax, Mom? You seem tired."

Anna dropped back into the chair and closed her eyes.

"Can you take care of dinner?" she asked Cassie. "Please? I don't think I can lift a finger."

Cassie dragged herself to her feet and shuffled into the kitchen, muttering something under her breath. She decided to make a quick salad. She rustled up her special Green Goddess dressing.

"Let's eat, Mom," she called out twenty minutes later.

Anna sat at the table and stared at the big plate of salad in front of her.

"What's this?" she asked. "Haven't you cooked anything?"

"This is a big salad, Mom. And the dressing's quite heavy too."

"I fancied a hot meal," Anna grumbled. "Too much to ask, I guess."

"You could have said so," Cassie shot back. "Do you want me to order a pizza for you?"

Anna shuddered.

"No thanks. I'll make do with this salad."

Cassie wished her mother wasn't so hard to please.

She put her head down and focused on cutting her salad into small bits. It was her version of a Cobb salad with boiled eggs, bacon, cherry tomatoes and plenty of ripe avocadoes.

Cassie watched as Anna worked through half her salad and buttered a second piece of bread.

"This is actually not bad," Anna said grudgingly. "I like the dressing."

"A chef from a big San Francisco hotel taught me his version of Green Goddess dressing," Cassie explained. "I made some changes to it."

"We can serve this at the café," Anna said. "It's that good."

"I thought you only wanted to sell cupcakes," Cassie countered.

Anna's eyes widened.

"We can start with baked goods. Then we could add some prepackaged stuff, or maybe add a salad bar."

"I think a salad bar is a great idea," Cassie nodded. "Don't think anyone's doing that kind of food in town. The diner's just a greasy spoon. The Tipsy Whale does great food but it's mostly carbs."

"Sounds like an odd combination," Anna mused. "Salads and dessert."

Cassie was glad to see some color back in her mother's face.

"How was your day, Mom?" she asked. "Anything interesting happen at the store?"

"I met Cody for lunch," Anna told her.

"I was in town for lunch too," Cassie said. "I'm surprised we didn't run into each other."

"Did you go to the diner?" Anna wanted to know. "That's where we were."

"I was at the Tipsy Whale," Cassie told her.

"Again?" Anna frowned.

"Wait till you hear this," Cassie said, leaning forward. "You'll be glad I went there."

Anna rolled her eyes and waited for Cassie to go on.

"Everyone was talking about this guy, your friend's son."

"Cody?"

"Right," Cassie nodded. "I don't think the natives like

him."

"What do you mean?"

"They all believe he is guilty, Mom. Not a single person was saying anything good about him."

"That's how gossip works," Anna said dryly. "People rarely have anything good to say about their neighbors."

"This was more than vague gossip," Cassie explained. "It seems this guy was very possessive about the dead girl."

"Maybe he was just being protective," Anna said, giving Cody the benefit of the doubt. "He was in love with her."

"I think he was smothering her. He wanted to keep her to himself."

"That doesn't bode well for the kid," Anna said worriedly. "What else did they say?"

"A couple of young girls were saying he was obsessed with the girl. He did creepy stuff, like holding her hand tightly all the time. As if she would run away if he let her loose."

"What was he so insecure about?" Anna wondered.

"What's he like?" Cassie asked. "I mean, were they well matched?"

"Cody's a good looking boy," Anna defended him. "Well behaved too. He was very popular in high school."

"So he's a jock?" Cassie countered. "Hmmm …"

"What's that for?" Anna asked.

"You met him today … what was your first impression, Mom?"

"It wasn't the first time I met him, Cassie. I've known him since he was a child."

"But you don't know the grown up version," Cassie pointed out. "Kids change, Mom. Teenaged Cody and present day Cody could be two different people."

Anna was quiet.

"I'm not talking about myself," Cassie said, reading her mother's mind. "Can we please focus on this kid?"

"He seemed sincere," Anna reflected. "He said he loved her. He even hoped to marry her. I think I can believe that."

"But?" Cassie prompted.

"He wasn't being completely honest," Anna mused. "I think he was hiding something."

"Did you call him out on it?" Cassie asked.

"Not this time," Anna said. "I didn't want to put him on his guard."

"That means you suspect him," Cassie pressed. "Do you think he is capable of hurting that girl?"

"I don't know, Cassie," Anna sighed.

"I thought you were on his side?"

"Not if he turns out to be guilty. I already told them that."

"What else do we know about this guy?"

"Vicki's very proud of him. She says he is a good student, always top of his class. She has high hopes for him."

"Like every mother on this planet," Cassie drawled.

"Vicki says he is the quiet type," Anna continued. "He's not the kind to pick a fight."

"That's completely opposite of what people were saying at the pub."

"Forget what people say," Anna snapped. "They have said plenty of unkind things about us over the years."

"Maybe we deserved them," Cassie said in a small voice.

"No one deserves being raked over the coals for the tough breaks they had in life," Anna said firmly.

Cassie stared at her empty plate, lost in thought.

"We did the best under the circumstances," Anna stressed. "Now how about some dessert? I need a sugar fix after the day I have had."

Cassie forced herself to smile.

"I ate all the tiramisu, Mom. But we have chocolate gelato."

"An Italian never says no to gelato," Anna said.

"Want to take a dip in the hot tub?" Cassie asked. "You look like you need it."

Anna thought of her aching limbs and agreed readily. Mother and daughter were soon out on the patio, relaxing in the giant jetted tub next to the swimming pool.

Cassie broached the subject of the café.

"You are not giving up yet, are you, Mom?"

"The girls and I have a plan," Anna said.

Cassie was skeptical as her mother talked about the proposed potluck.

"You think those signatures will matter?"

"Lara Crawford will have to cede to public opinion," Anna said confidently. "She can't go against the people. Not in a town like Dolphin Bay. Certainly not if she wants to be elected again."

"What of that nonsense about Daddy?" Cassie asked finally.

She had been brooding about it all day.

"We just sit tight," Anna said. "Don't worry, we'll be fine."

Cassie didn't share her mother's confidence but she smiled and said nothing.

Chapter 9

Cassie woke up feeling refreshed the next morning. She had slept well, heartened by spending some quality time with her mother. Her phone rang, signaling a video call. Cassie hit the green button when she saw it was Bobby.

"You awake, sweetie?"

"I'm just getting up, Bobby." Cassie let out a yawn. "I must look awful."

"You look beautiful 24x7," Bobby cooed. "Wait till you hear this …"

He launched into some gossip about a certain Hollywood star. She had been virtually unknown when Cassie was at the zenith of her career. But she had risen to the top fast, her ascent as meteoric as Cassie's fall had been.

"She wore that to the gala?" Cassie asked in a hushed voice. "Are you kidding me?"

"She never had your flair for fashion," Bobby dismissed. "You're still the queen, Cass. Everyone misses you. When are you coming home?"

"I am home," Cassie sighed. "The time's not right, Bobby. I need to be here to look after my Mom."

"Well, don't take too long," Bobby said, leaning closer to

the screen. "You know what they say, out of sight, out of mind."

"We'll talk about it when you come here," Cassie promised.

"Why don't you get a nice workout in, now that you're up?" Bobby asked. "We can do it together."

Cassie yawned widely.

"Maybe I'll go for a run."

"Do you promise?" Bobby asked sternly. "You need to stay fit, girl. Your arms are starting to look flabby."

"I could use a new weight training routine," Cassie pouted. "You really need to get here in person, Bobby."

Bobby promised to meet her soon and rung off.

Cassie spied the sheer white curtains at her window fluttering in the breeze and walked over. The spring morning was still cool. She breathed in the lingering scent of jasmine and smiled. Maybe a run wasn't such a bad idea.

She fished around in her closet and pulled out some running clothes. She put her hair up in a hasty pony tail. Five minutes later, she breezed into the kitchen.

Anna was fiddling around with the oven, baking a fresh batch of cupcakes.

"Good Morning, Mom," Cassie greeted her, pouring herself a glass of orange juice. "I'm going for a run."

She gulped her juice while Anna fussed about breakfast.

"I can eat later," Cassie said, rushing out of the door.

She decided to head to the Coastal Walk. It was a five mile stretch that ran along the bluffs, parallel to the bay. The path alternated between stunning views of the water and dense foliage from the towering pine and eucalyptus trees. Castle Beach Resort, a luxury retreat for the rich and famous, sat at one end of the Walk along with its award winning golf course. The other end led to Sunset Beach, a beautiful white sand paradise tucked away in a gentle cove.

Cassie walked to Bayside Books and cut onto the Coastal Walk. She headed north toward the resort, jogging slowly to warm up her body. She picked up speed as her limbs loosened, enjoying the salty breeze fanning her face. Spring was a beautiful time in Dolphin Bay and the cliffs were ablaze with wild flowers. Tourists came to town to gawk at the bright orange California poppies and the vibrant yellow mustard blooms that blanketed the ground.

Forty minutes later, Cassie slowed to a walk, taking deep breaths. The exercise had put her in a good mood. She was ravenous, looking forward to the tasty breakfast she was sure her mother would put together.

A voice hailed her. Cassie looked around and spotted a short, stocky man dressed in sweats waving at her.

"Hey Cassie!" the man beamed, jogging up to her. "Didn't know you were in town."

Cassie tried to remember how she knew the man.

"I'm Teddy," the man said, shaking his head. "Teddy Fowler. Don't you remember me?"

Cassie giggled. Teddy barely looked like the boy she had known in high school.

"Of course I remember you, Teddy," Cassie smiled. "But I didn't recognize you."

"It's been what, twenty years?"

"Something like that," Cassie nodded.

"You might have forgotten me, Cass, but I've followed your career. I have all your films on DVD. We have Cassie Butler movie night once a month."

"That's nice of you," Cassie mumbled.

She was beginning to remember bits and pieces about Teddy Fowler. He had asked her out a couple of times back in the day. Cassie had been going out with someone else at that time. It didn't seem like Teddy bore a grudge.

"Do you live in Dolphin Bay?" Cassie asked him.

"Some of us never left," Teddy said. "No complaints from me. I am happy here."

"Do you go for a run here every morning?" Cassie asked, pointing to the Coastal Walk.

"Come rain or shine," Teddy bobbed his head eagerly. "I never miss a day. Gotta keep in shape, you know. The job demands it. You should know. You Hollywood types are real sticklers for fitness."

"What do you do?" Cassie asked politely.

Teddy Fowler seemed to puff up with pride.

"I'm a detective with the local police force."

"No kidding!"

"I'm working on a very important case at the moment," Teddy preened. "A college kid was found murdered in the woods. You must have heard about it."

"I read something about it in the paper," Cassie offered. "So you are in charge of this murder investigation, huh?"

"That's right," Teddy said. "It's an open and shut case. That boy's going away for a very long time."

"You solved the case already?" Cassie asked, widening her eyes in wonder.

"We have pretty strong evidence," Teddy smiled. "Feels like it's been handed to us on a platter."

Cassie leaned closer to the detective.

"Go on, give me the scoop."

"We don't really discuss ongoing cases, but I guess I can tell you."

"My lips are sealed," Cassie promised him. "Who am I going to tell anyway?"

"We found the murder weapon right next to the body," Teddy said in a rush. "And guess what, it's got the suspect's finger prints all over it."

Cassie sucked in a breath.

"That sounds damaging."

"You bet it is," Teddy laughed. "We should be making an arrest soon. You will read about it in the Chronicle."

"I gotta go," Cassie told him. "It was nice catching up with you, Teddy."

"Hey, why don't we grab a pint sometime at the Tipsy Whale?" Teddy Fowler asked eagerly. "My wife would love to meet you. I've told her so much about you over the years."

"I'll think about it," Cassie promised.

"Come on, Cass, don't be shy!" Teddy pressed. "You are home now. I bet there's a lot of people from our class who will want to meet you."

Cassie remembered something more about Teddy Fowler. He was a bit of a leech. But he was harmless.

"Pick a day," she nodded. "I'll be there. Now I really have to go."

Teddy said goodbye and started jogging down the path. Cassie heaved a sigh of relief and dragged herself home. She was starving by the time she got there.

Anna had left a note for her on the kitchen table. A covered plate sat on the counter. Cassie lifted the top off eagerly and smiled when she saw the avocado toast and poached eggs. She polished off the food and poured herself a big mug of coffee.

Teddy Fowler had got her thinking. She took a quick shower and pulled out a couple of giant shoeboxes from her closet. They contained her most valued treasures, glimpses of her life in the past twenty years.

Cassie sat in the center of her bed, pulling stuff out of the boxes one by one, smiling at the glimpses of her life. There was a faded black and white photo of her with her first roommate in L.A. Cassie pulled out newspaper clippings depicting her going to lavish parties or receiving big awards. She stared at a photo of her holding the golden knight, the most coveted of all awards in the entertainment industry. Tears flowed down her cheeks as she thought of her past glory. Was Bobby right? Had everyone in Hollywood forgotten her? Was she supposed to spend the rest of her life in a small coastal town far away from the bright lights?

Cassie dumped everything back in the box and flung it into a corner of the room. She pulled out a bottle of vodka from underneath her bed and took a few swigs. Burying her head in the pillow, Cassie broke into sobs, blaming her fate and the world.

A few minutes later, the sobs turned into snores as Cassie settled into a disturbed sleep.

Chapter 10

Anna tasted her latest batch of raspberry chocolate cupcakes. The raspberry frosting was a bit tart, just as she liked it. She looked up as Cassie bounded into the kitchen, dressed in exercise clothes.

"Going somewhere?"

"Good Morning, Mom," Cassie greeted her with a broad smile.

She gulped some orange juice and went out for a run. Anna felt a ray of hope. Was her daughter finally getting out of her funk?

She cleared away all her baking stuff and started making breakfast. Cassie would be hungry when she got home.

An hour later, Anna pedaled her bicycle to the bookstore, enjoying the blooms in her neighbors' spring gardens. She glanced up at the magnolia tree before entering the store, noting with pleasure that some of the buds had opened and were looking very pretty, juxtaposed against the bright blue sky.

Anna finished her daily chore of dusting the shelves. She put some books back in their right spots and decided to take a look at the previous week's collections. She didn't enjoy keeping the books but it was a necessary evil for a small business owner. She couldn't afford to hire a full time accountant yet.

"Hola!" a voice called out just when she was beginning to make some sense of the numbers.

A hefty, heavily muscled man with close cropped hair walked in, wearing a sleeveless shirt stretched tightly across his formidable chest.

"Hi Jose," Anna said brightly. "How are you?"

"No time for small talk, Anna," Jose Garcia said, heading toward a window table.

Jose owned the corner store next to Bayside Books. He and Anna had an agreement. She was going to buy him out, knock down a wall and open her café in the new space.

Anna dreaded what was coming. She got up from her perch behind the cash register and sat down in front of Jose.

"Care for a cup of coffee? I was just about to make a pot."

"Thanks, but I am not here for coffee."

"What's on your mind?" Anna asked, steeling herself.

"Look, Anna. We've known each other a long time. That's why I cut you some slack. But I needed the money from the sale yesterday. When are you planning to close?"

"Soon," Anna said. "Very soon."

Jose scratched his head and stared right into her eyes.

"You're not being straight with me. I know the city didn't approve your café license."

"I have a plan, Jose," Anna pleaded. "I'll get the café approved. But I can't buy the space until then. Surely you see that?"

"I have another buyer lined up," Jose admitted. "He's offering cash upfront."

"Who is it?" Anna asked. "Some chain store from the big city?"

"Doesn't matter," Jose sighed. "I'm ready to retire. My cousin got a condo in Cabo last year and there's a unit for me right next to him. But I need to put in a deposit this month."

"I don't have that kind of cash," Anna admitted honestly. "Not right now. The bookstore hardly brings in any money."

Jose looked around in disgust.

"Aren't you tired of this dump? This guy from the city is willing to buy you out. He'll pay a bonus if he can get both units."

"Hold on a minute," Anna frowned. "I never said anything about selling this store."

"Suit yourself," Jose said, getting up. "Two weeks, Anna. We need to be in escrow by then or I am going with the other guy."

"Thanks Jose!" Anna said sarcastically.

Jose shrugged. "Hey! Nothing personal." He walked out of the store without a backward glance.

Anna wasn't in the mood to do the books after that. She went into the pantry and started a fresh pot of coffee. She had just finished adding an extra squirt of half and half to her cup when Julie walked in.

"I'll have one of that," she said, settling into an overstuffed armchair.

Anna was quiet as she handed over her friend's coffee.

"What's wrong?" Julie asked, picking up on Anna's distress immediately. "Are you sick? Is Cassie okay?"

"I'm fine," Anna assured her. "So is Cassie, as far as I know."

Julie sipped her coffee and waited for Anna to continue.

"Jose's given me an ultimatum. He has another buyer."

"What?" Julie cried. "Everyone in town knows you have a verbal agreement with Jose."

"It's some rich company from the city." Anna shrugged. "Can't say I blame him. I'm just running out of time."

"Do you have to open the café right away?" Julie asked. "Why can't you just expand the store?"

"The café is supposed to bring in the money," Anna sighed.

"That's what you should be focusing on then, Anna," Julie said. "Why are you wasting time playing Miss Marple?"

"I promised Vicki," Anna reminded her. "So? Have you learned anything new?"

"A little bit," Julie nodded. "I had a talk with Old Alfie. Had to promise him hardcover copies of my next five books."

"Did he know the girl?"

"He ran into her a couple of times. Alfie says Briana was a force to reckon with. She was super aggressive, it seems. Quite a go-getter."

"She doesn't sound like the kind to succumb to anyone," Anna reasoned.

"Exactly," Julie agreed. "You can say she was an unlikely candidate for murder."

"What about her parents?" Anna asked.

"The family moved here from the city. Her father worked in some factory. He met with a bad accident at work. He's in a wheelchair now. On disability."

"Sounds like he got a raw deal," Anna sympathized. "What about her mother?"

"The mother used to be a maid. She's been looking for a permanent job here, something that pays benefits. But she hasn't found one yet. She cleans people's houses. But I don't think that's steady work."

"Maybe we should give her a shot," Anna suggested. "It's time for spring cleaning anyway."

Julie didn't think much of the idea.

"What do we know about this woman? What if she's light fingered?"

"That's unfair, Julie," Anna protested. "You know nothing about her."

Julie ignored her and changed the subject.

"Didn't you have lunch with Cody yesterday? What's your take on him?"

"He's not being completely honest," Anna told her. "He insists he loved her, of course. And he says he is innocent."

"You don't sound convinced, Anna."

"We need to find out more about him, from people he's not related to."

"People other than Vicki, you mean," Julie said. "I agree."

"We also need more details about the crime itself," Anna continued. "All we know is Briana was found in the redwood forest. But how was she killed? What kind of weapon was used? Did they find anything else at the scene of crime?"

"You sound like a proper detective," Julie smiled. "Do you think the police will share all this information with you?"

"I doubt it," Anna said. "We might have to rely on the grapevine."

"You can talk to Gino Mancini," Julie suggested slyly.

"Gino's retired," Anna dismissed.

"No harm in asking," Julie said. "Gives you a reason to go talk to him."

"I don't need to drum up a reason," Anna said.

"Oh?" Julie arched her eyebrows.

"Actually, I went to the vineyard."

"What?" Julie exploded. "Way to bury the lead, Anna. Tell me everything. And don't skip the naughty details."

"It wasn't like that," Anna said indignantly. Then she smiled. "He invited me to a wine tasting later this month."

"The Spring Wine Tasting Event at Mystic Hill?" Julie asked. "It's a big thing, Anna. People from up and down the coast come to Dolphin Bay for it."

"So a lot of people turn up for this thing?" Anna asked.

"Yeah. Are you going as a special guest?"

"He didn't say," Anna said glumly. "I'm not sure if it was just a casual invite or ..."

"Or he was asking you out on a date," Julie finished for her.

"I barely know him, Julie," Anna said morosely. "I think he was just being polite."

"Do you like him, Anna?" Julie asked.

"I loved my John. I still love him. I never thought of another man since I met him."

"Relax!" Julie chided her. "No one's asking you to declare your undying love for this man. It's just a date, a glass of wine."

"I guess so," Anna said uncertainly.

"I can go with you if you want," Julie offered.

"I might take you up on it," Anna told her.

"Gotta go," Julie said. "My deadline's looming and I can tell you my editor is not happy with me."

Anna pointed to a stack of books next to the cash register.

"These are the books you wanted."

Julie picked them up, thanked Anna and went home.

Anna decided to make a list of things she needed to do next.

Chapter 11

It was a slow day at Bayside Books. Anna moped around after Julie left, ringing up purchases for a couple of customers. She picked up an old favorite, Little Women, and began reading some of her favorite passages from the book. The much thumbed copy was a clear indicator of how much Anna liked the book.

She looked up periodically as she flipped the pages, gazing out on the street. A couple of women she knew stopped on the sidewalk and peered inside the store. Anna smiled and waved at them. The women whispered something to each other and scurried off.

Anna started craving something starchy. She gathered her bag and went outside, salivating at the thought of some Lo Mein noodles from the local Chinese restaurant. Mrs. Chang, the proprietor of China Garden, greeted her with a smile.

"How are you today, Anna? You want some Kung Pao Chicken?"

"No chicken today, Mrs. Chang."

Anna made some small talk and decided to be greedy. She went for the large portion of noodles and went back to the bookstore, crumpling the fortune cookie before she attacked her food. She preferred to know what was in store before she shoveled a mound of greasy food into her stomach. Bad news gave her indigestion.

Anna couldn't make head or tail of the cryptic message. She threw it in the trash and started enjoying the hot noodles. She got engrossed in her book again and barely realized when she had worked through the entire carton.

The phone trilled just when she was nodding off. It was Mary.

"I had a busy morning," Mary explained. "Was on that video chat thingie for over an hour. Then I had to catch up with my chores."

Mary's grandchild had come down with a nasty bout of fever. She had been entertaining the toddler virtually, reading her favorite stories until she fell asleep. Mary's daughter lived in San Jose and Anna figured she would be making the 70-80 minute drive soon to go visit her.

"Mary, I've been thinking," Anna said, stifling a yawn. "Doesn't Ben know some police doctor?"

"Oh, you mean Rory?" Mary exclaimed. "Rory Cunningham. He's the one who cuts up people and conducts autopsies."

"So he's the medical examiner?"

"I guess so. Why are you suddenly asking after him?" Mary took her suspicion two steps ahead. "You're not sweet on him suddenly, are you, Anna? He's a strapping Scot. I think you'll make a great couple."

Anna let out a screech.

"You are way off track. I'm not looking for a man."

"Then why this sudden interest in Rory?" Mary demanded.

"It's for Cody, of course," Anna bristled. "Have you forgotten we are trying to save that poor boy?"

"Okay, okay," Mary soothed. "No need to get so snarky. Where does Rory Cunningham come in?"

"We don't know much about that girl," Anna started to explain. "How exactly did she die, for example? What happened to her and when? How long was she lying there?"

"You think Rory can answer all these questions?"

"That's his job, Mary. He will have some of the answers if not all."

"And why do you think he will tell us?"

"He will tell you," Anna stressed. "Because he knows you and because you will ask nicely."

Mary backtracked.

"I don't really know him that well, Anna. I mean, sure, he's Ben's poker buddy. I just ask him how he's doing. We talk about the weather or something. He asks about the grandkids. That's about it."

"That's more than enough," Anna said firmly. "Do you want to help or not, Mary?"

Mary took the bait.

"Let me give it a shot. But I don't have high hopes."

"It's been a slow day here," Anna said. "Why don't I close up early? We can meet at the Tipsy Whale in a couple of hours."

Mary sounded resigned. "Whatever you say, Anna."

"You'll be glad you helped. Trust me."

Anna hung up and walked around the store, trying to shake off her drowsiness. She tidied up the newspapers and wiped down the reading tables with disinfectant. She tackled the glass windows next.

The whitecaps rolled over the water in the distance. Wild poppies swayed in the breeze. Anna wondered what Cassie was up to. She picked up the phone and called her home phone. The answering machine kicked in after a few rings. Anna called Cassie's cell phone next but there was still no reply. Anna muttered a few choice words and berated her offspring. Then it was time to go meet Mary.

The Tipsy Whale was half full but people were streaming in steadily, eager to get their daily pint in before heading home. Murphy, the owner and bartender, greeted Anna cheerfully.

"Is that young lass of yours here to stay?" he asked.

Anna shrugged and headed toward a booth at the back. Mary was already there, sipping something dark with a straw.

"Let me guess...root beer?" Anna grinned, taking the seat before her.

"You're late," Mary noted.

"Last minute customer," Anna said lightly. "Never mind that."

Her eyes gleamed as she stared expectantly at Mary.

"So? Anything?"

"I spoke to Rory," Mary admitted. "He's a talker. Funny I never noticed that."

"Get on with it, Mary."

"I had to promise him a whole banana cream pie," Mary told Anna. "It seems he's partial to my pie. He says it's the best he's ever had. I think it's the caramel, you know. Just a tad bitter and salty is how I like it."

"Mary ..." Anna seethed.

"Calm down," Mary said lightly. "He did share a few things." She slurped her root beer and set the empty glass aside. "Briana was hit on the head with a bat. She died from the blow."

"How can he be sure?"

"They found a baseball bat right next to her, that's how."

"Oh." Anna was quiet.

"Things look really bad for Cody, Anna. The police think they have sufficient evidence against him. They are ready to bring him in."

"Why Cody? Anyone can swing a bat."

"Come on, Anna," Mary argued. "You know Cody was a star baseball player in high school. He almost went pro, didn't he?"

"He had to give up the game because of an injury," Anna sighed. "But I still say the bat could have belonged to anyone."

"There's more," Mary said. "Rory's not privy to that information but he heard some buzz."

"Thanks Mary. Did he say anything about when she died?"

"It was some time in the evening," Mary replied. "They have narrowed it down to a three hour window, I think."

"Hmmm. So what was Briana doing in the redwood forest that evening?" Anna mused.

"What next?" Mary asked.

"I need to go meet Briana's family."

"That sounds like a tough one. What will you ask them?"

"I haven't thought it through," Anna told Mary. "I am going to write down everything we know until now. That will give me a better picture of what needs to happen next."

Mary suddenly slapped the table with her hand.

"I completely forgot!"

"What now?"

"You remember I told you about that girl who's renting the room over my garage?"

"The one with the odd name?"

"Yes, Rain. I think it's a pretty name."

Anna rolled her eyes impatiently.

"She got hit by a car. And you'll never guess who was driving that car."

"Who?" Anna let out a wide yawn.

"Briana! I let Rain have some old copies of the Chronicle and she saw Briana's photo in it."

"So you are saying Briana was a bad driver?"

"Well, obviously," Mary said impatiently. "But isn't it funny?"

"I'm not laughing."

"That's not what I meant, Anna. It's odd. What a coincidence."

A couple of women walked up to their table. Anna knew one of them well. She lived down the street in the cul de sac. She had recently remarried, six months after her husband passed suddenly of a heart attack. The other woman was her sister and lived in a neighboring town. But she spent a lot of time in Dolphin Bay. She was the timid sort who nodded at everything her sister said.

"Hey Agnes," Anna greeted. "Your garden's looking pretty. Your roses have a chance at winning Best in Show this year."

"Don't you try to butter me up, Anna Butler," the woman hissed.

She was shorter than Anna with a shock of brown hair that looked odd against the deep wrinkles on her face.

"I know what you did. Heck, the whole town knows."

The sister nodded, chewing a strand of hair.

"Stop blathering, Agnes!" Anna snapped.

"Don't raise your voice, you … you murderer! We don't want your kind living on our street."

"But Anna's innocent," Mary exclaimed. "You are mistaken, Agnes!"

"That's not what Lara Crawford is saying," Agnes huffed. "You think the mayor would lie about something like this?"

"Lara Crawford has some kind of vendetta against Anna," Mary told her.

"That doesn't sound like Lara," Agnes said.

Her sister crept one step closer to her and nodded.

"Why isn't Anna defending herself?" Agnes asked with a sneer. "She's ridden with guilt, that's why."

"Are you done?" Anna asked. "Now leave me alone."

"You won't get away with it, Anna! I am going to warn everyone against you."

With that parting shot, Agnes strode away from their booth, her sister in tow.

Chapter 12

Cassie woke earlier than usual, feeling refreshed. She had slept through most of the previous day, barely getting up to eat some dinner. Her mother had thankfully left her alone.

There was a slight chill in the air and Cassie shivered as she pulled on her favorite old robe. It had cost a fortune once but Cassie had barely noticed. She trooped into the kitchen and went straight to the coffee pot. She added plenty of cream and sugar and sat at the table, sipping the delicious brew with her eyes closed.

"Did you get all the coffee? Again?"

Cassie looked up bleary eyed to find her mother scowling down at her.

"How many times have I told you to make a fresh pot?"

"Stop yelling, Mom. I have a headache."

It was the wrong thing to say.

Anna launched into a tirade, making Cassie's headache worse by the minute.

"Okay, okay," Cassie pleaded. "I'll make the coffee. Will that make you stop?"

She went to the sink, rinsed out the coffee pot, and refilled it.

"We are out of coffee," she groaned, staring into the empty canister.

"No, we are not," Anna sighed. "I grind the beans fresh every two days. Don't you know that by now?"

Cassie shrugged.

"So what now?"

Anna sat down at the table and folded her hands.

"Get the coffee beans from the pantry. Pull out the coffee grinder from that cabinet under the island. Grind them and then add them to the coffee maker."

"That's an awful lot of work," Cassie grumbled, searching the pantry until she found a container labeled 'coffee beans'.

"It's worth the effort, sweetie, like all good things in life."

"You don't have to go all philosophical on me, Mom."

"You're right," Anna said calmly. "I should just sit back and watch you squander your life."

"What have I done now?" Cassie asked wearily.

She gave up making the fresh coffee and went back to her own cup. It was already cold. She wondered if her mother had spotted the empty bottle beneath her bed.

"What are your plans, Cassie?" Anna asked. "What do you want to do with your life?"

"I'm an actress," Cassie said. "You know that, Mom."

"When was the last time you acted in a decent movie?"

Cassie thought her mother was being unfair. Hadn't she given up her life to come back home and nurse her through her illness? Cassie chose to ignore the fact that she had been virtually homeless when she came back to Dolphin Bay.

"I know you made a big sacrifice, Cassie," Anna said heavily. "You didn't have to do it but I really appreciate it."

"Are you turning me out, Mom?" Cassie asked, aghast. "Is that what this is about?"

"Of course not," Anna dismissed. "But you need to start thinking about your future."

"I'm reading a few scripts." Cassie was defensive. "I talk to my agent almost every day. This is just how the entertainment industry works, Mom. You have to wait for the right role to come along."

"Maybe it's time you gave it up then," Anna said.

"Give up acting?" Cassie's mouth dropped open. "No way, Mom."

Anna leaned forward across the table, trying to be more persuasive.

"Why don't you go visit the university? They have plenty of professional courses nowadays."

Cassie had dropped out of high school.

"You seriously think the university is going to accept me?"

"No harm in looking," Anna wheedled. "Once you take some courses, I could get you a steady job here in town."

Cassie couldn't imagine what kind of work her mother had in mind for her. But she decided to play along.

"I might head over there later."

"That's my girl," Anna smiled approvingly. "Can you make do with cereal today? I'm running late."

Cassie assured her mother she could fix her own breakfast.

A couple of hours later, Cassie drove to the campus, feeling a bit curious. At the very least, it would be good research for some future role.

Dolphin Bay University was a private institution. Admission there came with a hefty price tag. John Butler had taught history there for thirty five years. He had been honored with an emeritus status when he retired. Cassie vaguely remembered touring the campus with her father as a child, holding on tightly to his hand.

The campus bustled with activity. Groups of students hurried from one place to another, talking at the top of their voices. Some kids sat on the emerald lawns, reading giant books or discussing something.

Cassie felt the youthful energy ripple through the air. She spotted a group being led to a small walled garden and tagged along. The kids followed instructions given by a man wearing a white apron and plucked some fresh herbs. She followed them inside the building.

The man wearing the apron started explaining what each herb was and how it was best used. A young girl in a short haircut stood at the back, watching everything with interest. Cassie smiled at her shocking blue hair. It seemed a bit out of place in Dolphin Bay.

The instructor showed them how to cook a basic pasta dish. He offered a taste to his students. Cassie turned to leave.

The blue haired girl patted her arm.

"Don't leave yet. This is the best part."

"I don't actually go here," Cassie whispered.

"Neither do I," the girl said. "They won't mind."

Cassie ate a small morsel and widened her eyes in surprise. The instructor handed her a brochure listing various classes that were coming up in the fall. Cassie promised to get in touch if she had any questions.

She walked out with the blue haired girl a few minutes later.

"Are you a student here?" she asked the girl.

"I'm just passing through."

"Where are you going? We are not exactly a crossroads town."

"I am on a tour of the west coast," the girl explained. "Someone told me about the blooms here. So I decided to make a pit stop."

"How long are you staying?"

"I don't know," the girl laughed. "I'll hop on a bus or hitch a ride when I want to leave."

"Do your parents know where you are?" Cassie asked suspiciously.

The girl was short and skinny and her fresh face was completely unlined. Cassie pegged her age at sixteen.

"I'm legal," the girl said. "I don't need their permission. But yes, they know where I am."

"You remind me of myself," Cassie said wistfully. "I was young and fearless once."

"You don't look too old to me," the girl said kindly.

"Thanks. I'm Cassie Butler."

"Rain."

"Good luck on your travels, Rain."

Cassie said goodbye and looked around for a café of sorts. The day had cooled off and she needed something hot. She spotted a coffee cart under a tree and walked toward it.

The barista took Cassie's order for a nonfat mocha with extra cream without displaying any emotion. Cassie tapped her foot impatiently as she waited for her drink. She was beginning to wish she had brought a jacket.

Two girls huddled near the cart, sipping their coffees and whispering something. Cassie's ears perked up when she heard them mention the dead girl.

"She was trailer trash," one girl was saying. "You wouldn't know that by looking at her though."

"What are you saying?" the other asked in a scandalized tone. "She was such a diva. She had the best outfits, all branded stuff. How did she afford all that?"

"Her job took care of that," the first girl said, widening her eyes meaningfully.

"You don't mean …"

"I mean exactly that. She was one of Sherrie's girls."

The other girl had never heard of Sherrie. Cassie slid closer to them so she could get the scoop on Sherrie. She didn't learn much. The girls started discussing all the nice things Briana had owned and how much they must have cost. They both agreed she had been unfriendly and obnoxious.

"She got what was coming to her," the first girl said.

"Come on," the other girl protested. "She wasn't that bad!"

"Girls like Briana always come to a bad end."

They moved on to gossiping about some guy and walked away.

Cassie jumped when the barista called out her name. She took her coffee and stood there, thinking about what she had just heard.

There was a lot they didn't know about Briana Parks.

Chapter 13

Cassie spent the whole day on campus, stopping at one of the cafeterias for lunch. The amount of food on offer amazed her. She was yawning her head off by the time she reached home. It had been a while since she had been on her feet all day.

Anna was in the kitchen, cooking.

"Something smells nice," Cassie said appreciatively. "Is that our dinner?"

"You don't mind eating early, do you?" Anna asked. "I have to go out."

"I'm starving!" Cassie exclaimed. "Let me grab a quick shower, Mom."

Anna had finished setting the table by the time Cassie came back.

"What are we having?"

"Spaghetti and meatballs," Anna announced.

"With Nona's red sauce?" Cassie smiled brightly. "Yum!"

She loaded a bowl with salad and served herself a large helping of the pasta and meatballs.

"How was your day?" Anna asked.

"Tiring," Cassie grunted. "Tiring but awesome."

"What did you do?"

"I took your advice, Mom," Cassie said cheekily. "I went to the campus."

"You spent the whole day over there?" Anna was surprised.

"Pretty much," Cassie nodded. "It's huge, Mom. I barely checked out a few of the buildings."

"Anything interesting?" Anna asked lightly.

"Plenty!" Cassie said, pausing to take a big bite. "Did you know they have a culinary school? They have all kinds of courses. Wait till you see the brochures."

"You actually went inside a cooking school?" Anna asked.

"Yup! They have a Healthy Cooking course coming up in the fall. I might enroll in that one. They will give me a certificate."

"That's great, Cassie. You can help me create a Healthy Eats menu for the café."

"Any update on that, Mom?"

"I am meeting the girls tonight," Anna told her. "Mary has a plan. We need to put it in action."

"So you're going to meet the Firecrackers! Why didn't you

ask them over?"

"We need to meet Vicki," Anna explained. "It's going to be a tough visit."

"Why is that?"

"I am beginning to lose faith in her son," Anna admitted.

She told Cassie about Mary's conversation with Rory Cunningham, the medical examiner.

"They say a baseball bat was used as a weapon. Somehow, they are using it to implicate Cody because he used to play back in high school."

"That's not the only reason," Cassie said. "I forgot to tell you, Mom. I ran into Teddy Fowler from high school. He is the detective on Cody's case."

"You never mentioned that!"

"Sorry about that. But the point is, Teddy Fowler told me they found Cody's prints on the weapon."

"I don't like the sound of that, Cassie. I already told Vicki I won't defend her son if he's guilty."

"You might be hasty in judging him, Mom."

"What do you mean?"

"You know I spent the day walking around Dolphin Bay University? I heard a lot of stuff."

"What kind of stuff?" Anna asked wearily.

"Briana Parks had a lot to hide."

"Briana? You mean the dead girl?"

"Yes, Mom. She was flashy and aggressive. I don't think she had many friends."

"Julie says her family's going through a rough patch. They barely have two pennies to rub together."

"That's not what I heard," Cassie said. "Briana dressed in the latest fashion. She wore Louboutins. We know those don't come cheap. And she had a brand new car. Not just any car, a fancy convertible."

"How did she afford all that?" Anna cried.

"Funny you ask." Cassie smiled. "Do we have any dessert?"

"Chocolate cupcakes with raspberry chocolate swirl frosting. Tell me about Briana."

"Briana worked for someone called Sherrie."

"Does this Sherrie have some kind of business?"

"You could say that," Cassie chuckled. "It's the oldest business in the world."

Anna's mouth dropped open in amazement.

"Let me get this straight. You are saying Briana handed out favors in exchange for money?"

"That's one way of saying it."

"And this Sherrie got her into it?"

"That's what I heard."

"Is this girl new in town?" Anna asked. "How come I never heard of her?"

"She's a student, Mom, just like Briana or Cody. My guess is she lives on campus and keeps a low profile."

"Why does she do this kind of work?"

"Why do you think? For money, of course. College is not cheap, least of all DBU. It's one of the most expensive places in Central California."

"But it's got to be illegal!"

"I don't think the people involved care about the legalities. Who's going to tell? The girls need the money. And the creeps who hire them value their privacy."

"This changes things," Anna mused. "Briana could have gone out with any number of men."

"So Cody is not the only suspect, you mean."

"I wonder if Cody knew about this."

"You will have to ask him, Mom. But I am sure Briana was keeping it a secret."

"I don't think any young man will approve of his girl friend doing this kind of work," Anna reasoned.

"What if Cody found out and flipped?"

"It does give him a motive," Anna said, aghast.

"We know Cody was obsessed with Briana," Cassie reminded her mother. "And he's been known to be violent."

"We don't really know that," Anna protested. "What else do you know about this Sherrie?"

"Not much. But my guess is Briana wasn't the only one working for her."

"We need to find this girl," Anna said.

"Good luck with that," Cassie snorted. "How do you propose to do that? We don't know anyone who goes there."

"We know Cody," Anna reminded her. "Maybe he knows this girl."

"If you ask me, Briana would do her best to keep Cody and Sherrie apart. They represent parts of her life she would always want to keep separate."

"You may be right. But I need to know for sure."

"How do you know Cody won't lie?"

"I have to assume he's being honest with me," Anna sighed. "If he's not, we'll find out sooner or later."

"When are you going to meet Briana's family?" Cassie asked. "They might have something different to say about their daughter."

"Soon," Anna said. "I'm hoping Cody will introduce us."

"Does he know them well?"

"No idea," Anna shrugged.

She stood up and began clearing the plates.

"I'll take care of that, Mom," Cassie said.

"I'm just putting these in the dishwasher. Speaking of suspects, you know who's the most unlikely? Mary's lodger."

"What's a lodger?" Cassie asked.

Anna rolled her eyes.

"Some girl who's renting a room from Mary."

"What does this girl have to do with Briana?" Cassie asked, puzzled.

"Two days ago, Mary told me this girl had an accident. Today she tells me Briana was the one who almost ran the girl over."

"Was she hurt?"

"I think she had some minor bruises. She stumbled after trying to get out of the way."

"You think she had a grudge against Briana. So she went and killed her with a baseball bat. That's neat, Mom."

"It does sound farfetched when you put it that way," Anna said sheepishly.

"No, you're right. We need to consider every suspect. I don't know if this girl's motive is strong enough, though."

"It's strong if she's deranged."

"What do we know about her?" Cassie asked. "Where did Aunt Mary find this girl?"

Julie and Mary had been friends with Anna long before Cassie was born. They called each other soul sisters. So Cassie had called them Aunt or Auntie ever since she learned to talk.

"Mary puts up a hand written flyer at the post office or grocery store. This girl must have seen it and come knocking."

"That's not very safe," Cassie commented.

"Mary's been doing it for years. Most people coming through town are harmless."

"Can she keep an eye on this girl?"

"Mary likes to leave these people alone. She doesn't like to invade their privacy."

"We are not asking her to spy. Or maybe we are. She could pop in with some tea or cookies. Try to make the girl talk."

Anna laughed.

"I don't think Mary's cut out for something like that. Julie could do it in a heartbeat."

"You can all be present," Cassie offered. "Ask the girl over for lunch or dinner. You can size her up then, Mom."

"That's a good idea," Anna brightened. "Let me talk to Mary about it."

"How long will you be gone?" Cassie asked, yawning widely.

"I am going to be late," Anna told her. "Don't stay up, Cassie. We are planning to go play bingo after we meet Vicki."

"Have a good time, Mom. I'm going to watch some Netflix and turn in early."

Cassie went to her room to call Bobby, forgetting she had promised to clean up.

Chapter 14

Anna stared at the overcast sky outside her window as she made coffee the next morning. A light mist hung in the air, adding to the gloom.

Anna took her coffee out to the garden and thought of the day ahead of her. She had tried hard to hold herself together the past few days. But the insinuations and whispers had really rattled her. People she had known her entire life were beginning to doubt her character. If Lara Crawford continued to be on the warpath, Anna would never be able to hold her head up in town again.

Anna ignored the stab of pain she felt in her breast. She hadn't told Cassie or the Firecrackers about it, knowing they would make a fuss. Her doctor had told her it was part of the healing process.

Anna spent longer than usual talking to her plants. She looked at the pool wistfully and wished she could forget everything that ailed her and just lie in the sun like Cassie. Her stomach rumbled, signaling it was time for breakfast. Anna decided to fix some pancakes to cheer herself up.

Cassie breezed into the kitchen some time later, looking for coffee. Anna placed a stack of cinnamon blueberry pancakes before her.

"Pancakes!" Cassie squealed like a child. "Did you know I

ate pancakes only once in the past twenty years? That too because it was on set. They took the plate away as soon as the shot was finalized."

"I'm running late, Cassie. We can catch up later."

"What's bothering you, Mom? You don't look so good."

"I'm fine!" Anna said sharply. "Just fine."

Anna wove a scarf around her neck and mounted her bike. She pedaled furiously toward the bookstore, feeling guilty for being short with Cassie.

Anna realized how late she was when she spotted a couple of college kids waiting on the sidewalk outside the store. They needed some textbooks urgently. It turned out to be a busy morning and a steady stream of customers kept Anna on her feet. It was an hour before she got a chance to start the coffee.

Anna sat in the small chair behind the register, sipping her coffee and brooding again.

The front door shut with a bang, startling her. She stared at the woman who had stormed in. Her eyes breathed fire and all her wrath was directed at Anna.

"Who do you think you are?" the woman demanded, her hands on her hips.

Anna gauged the woman to be in her late forties. She wore a poorly fitting dress, stretched tight across her ample chest. Her hair hadn't seen any conditioner in a while. One of the heels on her worn out shoes was broken, making her limp.

Anna pasted a smile on her face and greeted the woman.

"How can I help you? Our bestseller section is right this way."

"I am not here to buy books, you hag."

Anna ignored the woman's threatening stance.

"This *is* a bookstore," Anna soothed, waving her hands around. "Are you here to read the newspapers? A lot of our customers like to do that."

"I'm here to warn you, you murdering witch."

"I think you should leave," Anna said, barely controlling her anger.

"I won't go until I have said my piece." The woman pursed her lips and glared.

"This is private property," Anna shot back. "If you don't get out of here in the next ten seconds, I am calling the police."

"We all know you have the police in your pocket," the woman sneered. "You got away with murdering your poor husband. Now you're helping that kid do the same."

Anna picked up the receiver and started dialing.

The woman collapsed into a chair and started sobbing.

"She was my only child. Can't you at least take pity on a grieving mother?"

"Who are you?" Anna asked, putting the receiver back in the cradle. "And what do you want from me?"

"I'm Pamela Parks," the woman spoke between sobs. "I'm Briana's mother."

Anna's face cleared.

"I am so sorry for your loss," she consoled. "I didn't know Briana but I would have loved meeting her."

"She was so young," the woman said, wiping her eyes with her hands. "She didn't deserve to be killed."

"No, she didn't." Anna handed her a box of tissues.

"Why won't you let the police do their job then?"

"I'm just trying to help," Anna said meekly.

Pamela cleared her throat.

"Word around town is you are meddling with the police. You are keeping them from arresting that boy."

"You have the wrong idea," Anna hastened to explain. "My goal is to find out what happened to Briana. If Cody is guilty, I will be the first one to turn him over to the police."

"Is that true?" Pamela asked hopefully.

"Of course," Anna nodded. "Cody and his mother both know that."

Pamela had simmered down a bit.

"I'm sorry I yelled at you," she apologized. "It's just ...I lost my baby girl. I've been crying so much I don't know which end is up."

Anna folded Pamela into a hug and stroked her back.

"I'm a mother too. I couldn't take it if anything happened to my daughter."

Pamela accepted the cup of coffee Anna offered.

"I'm glad you are here," Anna told her. "I wanted to ask you some questions about Briana."

Anna grilled Pamela for a few minutes, trying to get as much information as she could about Briana.

"My husband and I aren't doing too well," Pamela said hesitantly. "But we will pay you what we can. We just want justice for our daughter."

"You don't have to pay me anything," Anna assured her. "I started on this path to help Cody. I will see this through no matter what."

"I'm new in town but I have heard some pretty nasty rumors about you," Pamela said frankly. "I think someone wants to drive you out of town."

"They can try," Anna said. "I was born here and I am going to die here."

"Watch your back," Pamela warned as she said goodbye to Anna.

Anna's mood had improved considerably. She took up a feather duster and started cleaning the bookshelves. She looked forward to dozing in her chair once she was done.

The bell behind the door jangled again. Anna gaped at her next visitor with her mouth open.

A mop of golden hair topped a chiseled face with piercing blue eyes. Dressed in a three piece suit complete with pocket watch, the short man looked like he had walked out of one of Anna's books.

"Hello Anna."

"What are you doing here, Charlie?"

"Mother misplaced her copy of Pride and Prejudice. I was hoping to replace it."

"Let me check if we have it in stock," Anna said stiffly.

Charles Robinson was the owner of the luxury resort on the hill that marked one end of the Coastal Walk. Fernhill Castle had stood sentinel over Dolphin Bay for over a century. A young and ambitious Charles III or Charlie had converted it into Castle Beach Resort, a luxury destination for the rich and famous. The family had other business interests in the area and Charlie managed them all with a Midas touch. Charlie had never married and lived with his aging mother.

Anna pulled out a copy of the book from a shelf and handed it over.

"Actually, I'll take the whole set," Charlie said.

"You want the entire Austen collection?" Anna's eyebrows shot up.

"Why not?" Charlie shrugged. "It's all mother reads anyway. Most of the books are in tatters."

Anna pulled out the necessary books and placed them in a bag while she rang up the purchase.

"Why are you really here, Charlie?" she asked. "You never needed a book in the past twenty years."

Anna's husband John and Charlie Robinson had been inseparable at time. John was appointed to the Dolphin Bay Historical Society just around the time Charlie decided to convert the castle into a hotel. He wanted to list it as a historical property. John opposed some of the proposed renovations, most notably, the grand entrance foyer that Charlie wanted for the resort. John refused to approve the new design because it required tearing down the narrow but original door.

The issue escalated and caused a rift between the two friends. John Butler died before they could ever reconcile.

"I am hearing the rumors, Anna, just like everyone else in town."

"And you believe them?"

"You have a powerful opponent, Anna," Charlie said softly. "You need powerful friends."

"What are you saying?" Anna asked.

"I should have made up with John years ago, but I can't bring back the past. I am here to support you, Anna."

"So you believe I am innocent?"

"I never doubted it for a second."

"Thanks, Charlie. That means a lot."

Charlie frowned.

"I came to warn you, Anna. Some people are starting to believe the rumors. Get ready to fight."

Chapter 15

The Firecrackers huddled together in the China Garden restaurant. Anna had called Julie and Mary the moment Charlie Robinson left.

"I'm calling an urgent meeting," she told Julie. "Get Mary and come to the Chinese restaurant. Now!"

She had locked the bookstore in the middle of the day and rushed over to the restaurant, overwhelmed by the morning's events.

"What's got you all hot and bothered, Anna?" Julie demanded as soon as she sat down.

Mary slid in next to her, giving Anna a concerned look.

"Do we need to go to the doctor?" she asked Anna.

"For the hundredth time, I'm fine!" Anna sighed in frustration. "You girls have got to stop thinking there's something wrong with me."

"But you went through a major surgery just weeks ago," Julie argued. "You're still recovering, Anna."

"We worry about you," Mary added.

"I appreciate that," Anna stressed. "I really do. But I can't be back to normal until the people around me, you girls and

Cassie, stop treating me like an invalid."

"That's crap!" Julie snapped. "If we want to treat you with kid gloves, we will."

Anna's eyes narrowed and she looked like she was about to explode.

"Let's change the subject," Mary pleaded, trying to maintain the peace as usual. "Why don't we order lunch first?"

Julie wanted Sichuan Chicken, Mary went for the Beef and Broccoli and Anna grudgingly ordered the Cashew Chicken. They each ordered an egg roll as an appetizer with their meal.

Anna had simmered down by the time she took a few bites of her egg roll.

"I didn't mean to shout at you," she said.

"We worry about you because we love you," Mary said softly, tearing up.

Anna's eyes welled up too and they dabbed at their eyes with a tissue while Julie rolled her eyes. She wiped her own eyes with the collar of her plaid shirt.

"It's been a wild day," Anna told them. "First I got a visit from Briana's mom."

"What did she want?" Julie inquired.

"She warned me against aiding the guilty party. She's convinced Cody is guilty."

"Isn't everyone?" Julie shrugged. "That kid has the odds stacked against him."

"She calmed down after a while and we talked about Briana."

"Did you learn anything new?" Mary asked.

"We know a bit about Briana's life now," Anna said. "She was an English major. Her mother Pamela told me they were proud of what she had achieved. Briana was working her way through college and supporting her parents as much as she could."

"What about her relationship with Cody?" Julie asked. "Did they know about him?"

"They must have," Anna said. "Pamela told me Cody loved Briana a lot but he was clingy. He wanted to know where she was at all times."

"What's the matter with kids these days?" Mary wondered. "They are talking with each other on that video thing all the time. And they are still insecure."

"Pamela said Cody sent text messages to Briana every few minutes. Her phone would ring if she answered a few seconds late. One time she was so tired she switched her phone off. Cody was banging on their door fifteen minutes later, worried there was something wrong with her."

"That might be a bit obsessive," Julie mused. "But it also shows he was crazy about her."

"What else?" Mary asked. "Did Briana have any other

friends?"

"Pamela mentioned a girl," Anna nodded. "She helped Briana get a job and introduced her to a professor in her department. He took special interest in her, acted as her mentor."

"She was doing well in every aspect of her life," Mary noted.

"That's debatable," Anna said.

She told them what Cassie had learned on her visit to the local university.

"Now we're talking," Julie said. "This is the kind of dirt we need."

Mary looked scandalized.

"Surely things weren't that bad!"

"Old Alfie told me he saw her mother at the food bank," Julie told them. "If that's true, I don't think Briana had a choice."

"Let's not be hasty in judging her," Anna protested.

"I'm not judging," Julie argued. "I'm saying they were in dire straits. Briana rose to the challenge. I actually admire her for it."

"Does her mother know what kind of job she had?" Mary asked.

"She didn't mention it," Anna said. "I don't see any point in telling her now. Why add to their misery?"

Julie and Mary both agreed.

"What does Cody feel about all this? Did he even know about her job?"

"I talked to him today," Anna said. "I warned him about the fingerprints."

"What was his bat doing at the scene of the crime?" Julie asked.

"He doesn't know. He can't remember where he saw it last."

"Do you believe him?" Mary asked.

"I'm not sure," Anna admitted. "He may be lying about the bat, but I think he didn't know about Briana's work. He said she was very secretive about it. He sounded frustrated."

"Isn't the bat the most important?" Julie quizzed. "It's the crucial piece of evidence that's going to get him arrested."

Mrs. Chang brought over their food. The girls stopped talking for a while and attacked the food. Anna came up for air after she had wolfed down half her chicken.

"Honestly, I don't know what to think any more. I can't make sense of anything."

"You're not giving up yet, Anna," Mary said. "Think of it

like a jigsaw puzzle. First you need all the pieces. Then you need to assemble them to get the complete picture."

"That's just it," Anna sighed in frustration. "I'm not even sure I have all the pieces."

"We need a systematic approach," Julie lectured. "That's what I do when I am plotting a book."

"I think this is more serious," Mary argued. "A young man's life is at stake here."

"All I mean is, we need to be logical. It's not going to be easy."

"I'm going to write down everything I know when I get back to the store," Anna said. "Then I will work on filling in the blanks."

"I think the bat is important," Julie stressed. "We can't refute where it was found and we can't deny it's covered in Cody's prints."

"I'll keep that in mind," Anna promised.

"Who was your other visitor?" Julie asked. "You said Pamela Parks was the first one."

Anna skimmed over Charlie Robinson's visit.

"That sly fox!" Julie exclaimed. "What does he want now?"

"I think it was very kind of him," Mary said. "He's right, you know. He does have a lot of clout."

"Even he can't stop all the hurtful gossip," Anna murmured.

"Just let it roll off your back," Julie said grimly.

"She's right," Mary said. "Don't feed the fire. Just ignore them and walk away."

"You saw how Agnes was acting that day," Anna reminded them. "They are saying things to my face."

"Just remember you are not alone," Julie soothed. "We are going to be right beside you no matter what."

"Thanks, girls. Most of my strength comes from you."

Anna placed her hand on the table and Julie and Mary gripped it tightly.

"How's your sleuthing coming along?" Julie asked, turning around to face Mary.

Mary shuddered.

"This is the first and last time I am going snooping for you. I don't think my poor heart can take it again."

"Did you find something?" Anna asked eagerly.

"I've never violated anyone's privacy like this," Mary frowned.

"Was it worth it?" Julie asked. "Spill it, sister."

"I went in on the pretext of vacuuming the room," Mary

told them. "Rain was just going out. She told me she would run the vacuum cleaner when she got back."

"Then?" Anna asked.

"I told her it was part of the rent. She believed me and left. She seems like a well brought up kid. The bed was made and there wasn't anything lying about. So I opened a few drawers."

Mary paused to take a breath.

"I found a lot of brochures, the kind they hand out to tourists at the visitor center. One of them had Briana's name written on it along with a phone number and an email address. At least, it looked like a phone number."

Julie and Anna stared at Mary, wide eyed.

"So this girl Rain or whatever her name is met Briana?" Julie asked.

"We don't know that," Anna said.

"How else did she get her number?" Julie shot back. She turned toward Mary again. "Does she know Briana's gone?"

"She does," Mary nodded. "I gave her the Chronicle, remember? She's read the news about Briana's death."

"So what is this kid doing with a dead girl's contact information?" Anna asked.

None of them had an answer for that.

Chapter 16

Anna walked back to the bookstore after lunch, determined to come up with some answers. Lara Crawford stood outside the Tipsy Whale, talking to a group of local women. One of the women glared at Anna and shook her head in disgust. Anna ignored them and went inside the store.

She made a fresh pot of coffee and pulled out a brand new writing tablet from a box at the back of the shop. She started writing down all the facts she knew about Cody and Briana. She listed out the possible motives someone may have had against Briana. She had an epiphany of sorts and wrote down possible motives against Cody. Half an hour later, she sat back with a groan and stared at the pages she had filled.

Anna felt she was still going around in circles.

The bell over the door jingled and a gray haired woman wearing thick horn rimmed glasses walked in. Anna's face lit up when she saw her.

"Hey Sally," she greeted. "Long time no see."

Sally Davis taught mathematics at Dolphin Bay High. A spinster whose life revolved around her job, she had a secret love for historical romances. Bayside Books was her favorite place to hang out when she was not at school. Anna was used to setting aside a copy of the latest releases for her.

Sally's cheerful countenance was nowhere in sight that day.

"How are you holding up, Anna?" Her voice quivered with barely controlled rage.

"I am good, Sally," Anna said, finally noticing the woman's distress. "But you don't look too good to me."

"I hope you don't think I am on her side," Sally pressed. "I never pay attention to such drivel."

"What on earth are you talking about?"

"That vile woman – Lara Crawford. I was having lunch with some ladies from the Booster Club. She just cornered us and started spouting some nonsense about you."

"I know what she's saying, Sally," Anna said grimly. "But thanks for letting me know."

"I don't believe her one bit," Sally Davis said stoutly. "I have known you and John for years. I know how devoted you were to each other. No way you harmed a hair on his head."

"It's nice to see someone believes in me," Anna said sincerely.

"Of course I believe in you," Sally said, gratefully accepting the cup of coffee Anna handed her. "And I'm not the only one. This town knows how much you have done for the less fortunate."

Anna hung her head.

"They have short memories, Sally."

"Lara Crawford may be a smooth talker, but not everyone is gullible, Anna. I am here to remind people of what you have done, all the kids you have helped. I might call in your kids if need be."

"Don't drag them into this," Anna said in alarm. "They are busy living their lives."

"Lives they would never have had without you," Sally said in earnest. "You and John did a lot for those kids. You trusted them and believed in them. Most of all, you loved them when no one else would."

Anna's cheeks turned pink.

"We did nothing great," she protested. "Cassie was gone and there was a void in our lives. We had an extra room and enough to feed an extra mouth or two."

"So do thousands of people in this country," Sally Davis argued. "But they don't choose to be foster parents."

"It's all in the past now, Sally. John's gone. I'm not sure how many Christmases I'm going to see."

"A few dozen, at least," Sally Davis clucked. "You're a survivor, Anna. This kind of pessimistic talk doesn't suit you."

"I'm tired, Sally," Anna admitted. "The café was the only thing that kept me going through my long treatment. It's been my dream for so long. But it's never happening if I can't get a license."

"Mary told me all about it," Sally said. "I am already talking to the teachers at school. We'll be here at the potluck with a pen in our hands, ready to sign that petition."

"I appreciate that. I'm going to need all the support I can get."

Sally chatted for a few more minutes while she sipped her coffee. Then she had to rush back to school.

Anna walked around the store, rearranging books and putting them back on the right shelves. She found a wine magazine on the reading table and smiled broadly. She placed a call to Cassie and called her over.

Anna put the 'Be Right Back' sign in the window and stood under the magnolia tree, hoping to flag her daughter down before she pulled into the parking lot.

"Can you give me a ride?" she asked before Cassie rolled to a stop.

"Where to?" Cassie sulked. "This better be important, Mom. I was about to call my agent."

Anna didn't understand why Cassie said that all the time. Did such a person really exist? Why did Cassie need to call him or her every day?

"I have to go to Mystic Hill," Anna told her. "Do you know the way?"

Cassie jabbed some buttons on the map in the dash and started with a lurch. Anna clutched the door with her hand as Cassie sped up the hill.

She felt a bit lightheaded when she climbed out of the car fifteen minutes later.

"Go back to the store and stay there until I get back."

Cassie gave her a mock salute and turned the car around with a screech of tires.

"Be careful on those curves," Anna called after her.

Gino Mancini had come out to welcome Anna.

"This is a nice surprise," he said.

Anna admired his dimples and decided his smile was genuine.

"I should have called ahead," she winced.

"No need," Gino said, offering his arm. "The door's always open for my friends."

Anna entered the familiar warm sitting area and let Gino lead her to a really comfy armchair. He excused himself and came back bearing a tray with two wine glasses. A plate of biscotti rested on the side.

"Isn't it a bit early for wine?" Anna murmured.

"Mystic Hill is a winery," Gino laughed. "Wine is our default drink."

Anna let him pour the golden liquid. She watched him swirl the wine around in his glass and take a sniff. She copied his actions and took a small sip.

"It's nice," she approved. "I don't know much about wine. I just can't care about the ones that taste like vinegar."

"Mystic Hill wines will never taste like that," Gino said proudly.

Anna dipped the pistachio studded biscotti into her wine and munched on it. Then she mentioned Briana's murder.

"I'm having a hard time making sense of it all," she admitted. "I really need some help."

"Have you established a timeline?" Gino asked. "Start with a few hours before the crime was committed. Try to find out where every suspect was at that time."

"You mean check on everyone's alibi?" Anna nodded.

"They can't always pinpoint the exact time," Gino told her. "You will have to start with a wide window and then try to narrow it down as much as possible."

"You make it sound so easy," Anna gushed. "I suppose that's your experience talking."

"As police officers, we are trained to work methodically," Gino agreed. "But an amateur can bring a fresh perspective."

"You mean I should keep throwing the pasta at the wall until something sticks?" Anna blushed.

"Have I offended you?" Gino asked, alarmed. "I didn't mean to mock you, Anna. I hope you believe that."

"I wouldn't blame you," Anna said. "I've got some cheek, huh? Coming here, asking you to help me."

"I'm flattered you thought of me," Gino said. "Forget all this. Why don't you stay for dinner? I'm making pot roast."

Anna knew Gino lived alone. His wife had run away with a man years ago, abandoning him and the kids.

Anna didn't hide her surprise.

"I thought a big vintner like you would have a cook."

"You're right," Gino laughed. "But I like to potter around in the kitchen every now and then. Keeps me young, you know."

"Thanks for your tempting offer," Anna said shyly. "Maybe some other time?"

"You have an open invitation," Gino murmured. "My kids rarely have time for a visit. My nephew is the only one who takes pity on me sometimes."

"I would be honored to have dinner with you, Gino," Anna said. "And it won't be a chore."

Gino offered to drive Anna back to town and she accepted. The sun was going down over the bay when Gino reached the corner of Main Street. Flames of red and orange shot up in the sky, looking like a massive work of art. People milled around on the Coastal Walk, enjoying the view.

Anna thanked Gino and stood waving until his truck was out of sight. She was in high spirits when she went inside her store. The scene that greeted her instantly spoiled her mood.

Cassie leapt up from the chair behind the cash register as soon as she saw Anna.

"I'm off, Mom," she said, slinging her bag on her shoulder. "See ya."

Anna shook her head in disbelief at the mess around her. Books lay half open, piled on corner tables and chairs. Some books lay on the floor, as if they had been thrown off the shelves. A pile of magazines sat in an untidy heap on Anna's desk.

She started tidying up, wishing she had accepted Gino's offer and stayed at the vineyard for dinner.

Chapter 17

Cassie grabbed her bag and rushed out of the bookstore as soon as she saw her mother come in. She had been tired of being cooped up inside the store. Missing her afternoon nap had made her cranky.

Cassie decided to cook something nice for dinner and headed toward Paradise Market. The only grocery store in Dolphin Bay, it stocked much more than fresh produce, aiming to pander to the quirkiest needs of its customers. Cassie wasn't a great cook but she made some things well. Her second husband had been really good at cooking Chinese food. She had learned a basic dish from him, fried rice. It was her favorite comfort food.

Picking up a basket from a pile, Cassie began loading it with fresh vegetables.

"Cassie Butler shopping for vegetables!" a loud voice exclaimed. "Now I've seen it all."

Cassie turned to see Ted Fowler grinning at her, standing behind a loaded shopping cart.

"Don't you have minions to do this kinda work?" Teddy pressed.

Cassie decided the bright wide eyed expression on Teddy's face was genuine.

"I don't have any staff here," she gave a brief but honest answer.

She didn't have any staff anywhere but Teddy didn't need to know that.

"I told my wife about you," Teddy said. "She wants to get a haircut before we meet at the pub for drinks."

He leaned forward and whispered in Cassie's ears.

"Ain't gonna make her prettier than you."

"How's work, Teddy?" Cassie asked smugly. "Made any progress?"

"We are tying up the loose ends," Teddy bragged, "prepping for a big arrest. You'll read about it in the Chronicle soon."

"That's what you said last time," Cassie needled. "I think you have the wrong guy. The police are just stalling because they are stumped."

Teddy became flustered.

"Come now, Cassie. You stay out of it."

"Have you looked into your victim, Teddy?" Cassie asked, setting her basket down.

Her arm was beginning to ache from all the weight.

"Briana Parks was hiding something."

"How dramatic," Teddy laughed. "I guess you Hollywood types are used to making a big fuss out of everything."

"I'm telling you the truth," Cassie sighed. "The police would know that if they were doing their job."

"I'm the detective on this case," Teddy said grimly. "And I've made sure we covered our bases. If you have any information for the police, you better come clean, Cassie."

"I'm not hiding any big secrets," Cassie sizzled. "You just have to ask around."

"Stop talking in riddles, Cass. If you have something to report, just do it."

"Forget I said anything," Cassie said, picking up her basket.

She turned around and started walking toward the rotisserie chicken. It was the essential ingredient in her quick and easy dish.

Cassie lugged her grocery bags across the street as she walked to the parking lot, ignoring the pain in her knee. The doctor had told her it was early onset arthritis and it would only get worse. Bobby had given her a set of exercises to strengthen the knee and warned her to do them a few times a day. Cassie wasn't sure they helped at all.

The lights blared inside Bayside Books. Cassie could see her mother walking around, straightening things, getting ready to close. She looked preoccupied. Cassie decided she would talk to her mother about it at dinner.

Cassie had the food on the table by the time Anna got

home. She had even squeezed in a shower and tidied everything up.

Anna sat down with a sigh and pulled the lid off a large pan.

"What's this?" she grumbled. "Rice?"

"It's my special Chicken Fried Rice," Cassie said eagerly. "I made some teriyaki sauce to go with it."

"But I had Chinese food for lunch!"

"You could have mentioned that before!" Cassie exclaimed, feeling deflated.

"I didn't know you were cooking," Anna mumbled.

"We are having fried bananas with ice cream for dessert," Cassie cajoled. "You love them, don't you?"

"With caramel sauce?" Anna asked hopefully.

"Of course!"

"I guess I can eat fried rice."

She took a bite and beamed at Cassie.

"This is good. Nothing like what they serve at China Garden."

Cassie accepted the olive branch her mother offered and cracked a smile.

"How was your day, Mom? Find anything new?"

"Not really. But Gino gave me some excellent advice. I am putting together a timeline of what happened the day Briana died."

"But she was found a day later, right? So you are just guessing here."

"It's not all guesswork," Anna explained. "They can tell the approximate time give or take a few hours."

"A lot can happen in that time," Cassie mused. "Dolphin Bay isn't like L.A. You can drive around town multiple times in an hour."

"You're right. That's why Mary's talking to Rory Cunningham again. He's the guy who does the autopsy. She's going to ask for his best guess."

Cassie hid a smile as Anna took a third helping of rice, scraping the pan clean. She was happy to see her mother's appetite was back to normal.

Cassie stood up to fry the banana fritters. It didn't take her long. She plated their desserts and sat down again, heartened by the wide smile that lit up Anna's face. The Butlers had a big sweet tooth and they never said no to dessert.

"You need to find out more about Briana," Cassie said, taking a big bite of ice cream. "From what I heard on campus, she wasn't very popular with the other girls."

"Girls can be catty," Anna said. "I bet they were jealous of her looks and her money."

Cassie could easily relate to that.

"There was this girl I used to share an apartment with back in the day," Cassie told her mother. "I thought she was my best friend. We auditioned for the same part. She was very supportive when neither of us got the part. Then the studio called. They couldn't make it work with the girl they had chosen. I had been their second choice. You wouldn't believe the stunts my friend pulled."

"That was the part that landed you the Oscar, wasn't it?" Anna beamed.

"How did you know that?" Cassie asked, surprised.

As far as Cassie knew, her parents had never been keen about her film career.

"I kept track of you, sweetie," Anna said. "The tabloids made a big deal of your falling out with this girl."

"I was devastated," Cassie confessed. "I never thought she would betray me like that."

They talked about the hard lessons life had taught Cassie after she left home.

"My point is," Anna stressed. "Everyone's jealous of the popular girl. Those girls might have gossiped about Briana or spread nasty rumors about her. But that doesn't mean they would actually harm her."

"What about that girl Briana was working for?" Cassie asked suddenly.

"You mean the girl who was sending her on those assignments?" Anna cringed. "I forgot all about her. What was her name?"

"Cherry," Cassie said. "No. Sherrie. Something like that."

"This girl must have taken some kind of commission. She was making money off Briana."

"What if they had a falling out?" Cassie asked. "Or what if Briana got big ideas? She might have wanted to cut this girl out of the equation."

"So what? She bumped her off?"

"We thought she managed a bunch of girls, not just Briana. She might have wanted to make an example out of her."

"You make her sound like a gangster," Anna scoffed. "Isn't she a student at DBU?"

"That's my guess. I don't know for sure."

"We need to track this girl down," Anna said thoughtfully. "She might be able to set some things straight."

"Have you talked to Cody?" Cassie asked. "How's he holding up?"

Anna shrugged.

"He's not doing good according to Vicki. But it could all be an act."

"So you think he did it?" Cassie asked, astounded. "Looks

like you have made up your mind, Mom."

"I haven't," Anna insisted. "But I don't blindly believe in Cody anymore."

"What's your next move going to be?"

"Honestly, I don't want to think about this now. I think I might turn in early."

"I'll bring you some warm milk later," Cassie promised. "With nutmeg. It will help you sleep."

"What did I tell you about coddling me?"

"I'm not," Cassie said casually. "Bobby told me about this warm turmeric milk with nutmeg. They call it golden milk. It's the latest fad in Hollywood. It's great for your immunity and your skin. It's also supposed to cure a sore throat. And it's, err, it's supposed to kill cancer cells."

"Imagine that!" Anna smirked. "If only I had drunk this magic milk two years ago. I would never have had cancer!"

Cassie smiled indulgently as her mother went to her room. She had forgotten what a spitfire her mother was. The past couple of years had dampened her spirits but Cassie was glad to see Anna getting some of her spunk back.

Chapter 18

Anna woke up refreshed after a good night's sleep. She would never admit it to Cassie, but the warm milk had worked liked a charm. Anna sat out on the patio, drinking her coffee and admiring the flowers in her garden. It had been her husband John's pride and joy. She had employed a gardener for the past couple of years and tried to keep the garden flourishing just as it had in John's day.

An hour later, Anna was pedaling her bike to Bayside Books. Main Street was bustling with shoppers. Anna went in and started her daily chores. A few of the Main Street shoppers came in to browse. A couple of new bestsellers were making waves and everyone wanted a copy.

Anna was just sitting down with a cup of coffee when Julie breezed in.

"You're taking me out to lunch," she announced.

"Is it that time yet?"

"It will be, by the time I have finished telling you my story."

"What have you done now, Julie? I thought you had a class today?"

Julie taught a basic creative writing seminar at Dolphin Bay University. She wasn't very keen on it but the college had begged and pleaded until she said yes.

"That's where I am coming from," Julie said eagerly. "And you'll never guess what happened."

"What?" Anna asked wearily.

"I was going through the list of students who take my class…" Julie shook her head the moment Anna opened her mouth. "No, there are over fifty students in the class and I don't know all their names."

"Go on."

"Who do you think I found on that list? Briana. Briana Parks."

"Didn't someone say she was an English major? I suppose it's natural she might want to take a creative writing class."

"I must have seen her in class sometime," Julie mused. "But of course I didn't know who she was then. Nor did I know what was gonna happen to her."

"Are you leading up to something, Julie?"

Julie bobbed her head eagerly.

"I talked about what had happened to her and asked the kids if they wanted to say something. You know, like a eulogy."

"That was nice of you. Did anyone come forward?"

Julie shook her head.

"Not immediately. But get this. One of the kids came over to talk to me after class."

"What did he want?"

"I think he just wanted to gossip. He started talking about Briana. How she was always well groomed, her shiny new car…"

"We know all that," Anna said impatiently. "Did he actually say anything new?"

Julie smiled coyly.

"This kid said Briana got along really well with the professors. You can say she was their pet."

"Every teacher has some protégé. My John was always impressed by the brightest students in the class."

"The way this kid was talking, Briana wasn't just a protégé."

"Oh?" Anna quirked an eyebrow in question.

"Briana openly flirted with the teachers. This kid said she would do anything to get a good grade."

"That sounds a bit mean," Anna said. "How well do you know this kid anyway? Why is he badmouthing a dead girl?"

"I never noticed him before," Julie admitted.

"He could be after a good grade himself," Anna remarked.

"So you think he was saying all this just to get my attention?"

Julie sat down, looking like a deflated balloon.

"Maybe he wasn't lying outright," Anna suggested kindly. "He could have been stretching the truth."

"I think we know Briana was ambitious to a fault. She was prepared to do anything to get ahead in life."

Anna bunched her eyebrows together.

"Was Cody aware of this side of her personality?"

"She might have acted all sweet and coy with him," Julie said. "The real Briana wasn't the person he fell in love with."

"You understand we are just speculating here?" Anna said. "We need to talk to more people who knew Briana."

Julie shook her head.

"I have had enough for one day. I'm starving. Let's head out to lunch."

Anna went to the window and flipped the 'Open' sign to 'Closed'.

"Why don't you call Cassie over?" Julie asked. "We can grab a sandwich for her on our way back."

"I'd rather not," Anna dismissed. "You wouldn't believe the mess she made the last time she was here."

"Cut her some slack, Anna. So she's not a neat freak like you. She's here, isn't she?"

"Why is she here exactly?" Anna asked. "Shouldn't she be back there in Los Angeles, looking for work?"

"You know she came here to take care of you."

"She can go back now," Anna grumbled.

"You know what I think about that," Julie said. "You are getting used to having her around."

Anna's mouth settled into a pout. She slung her handbag on her shoulder and started walking toward the door.

"You are afraid she will leave again," Julie continued. "Am I right, or am I right?"

"Where do you want to eat?" Anna asked, refusing to take the bait. "I fancy a nice juicy burger."

Julie followed Anna out of the door, muttering to herself. They walked around Bayside Books to Ocean Avenue toward the Yellow Tulip Diner.

"Slow down, Anna," Julie called. "I can't keep up with you."

Anna turned around to glare at Julie and almost walked into someone.

"Oops!" she exclaimed, staring at the golden haired man smiling back at her.

Anna jumped as his arms came around to steady her.

"Are you okay, Anna?" Charlie Robinson asked.

He was wearing a golf outfit complete with a jaunty flat cap. His icy blue eyes narrowed as he nodded at Julie. There was no love lost between them.

"I'm sorry," Anna apologized. "I guess I wasn't watching my step."

"No harm done," Charlie smiled. "Can I escort you ladies somewhere?"

"Oh no," Anna burst out. "We were just going to grab a bite."

"Thanks for the kind offer," Julie said stiffly.

"I'm heading back home myself," Charlie offered. "Why don't you come to the resort for lunch? My treat. I am trying out a new chef and I would love to get your opinion, Anna."

"We are in a hurry," Julie interrupted. "And we are meeting someone else."

Anna nodded vigorously.

"Thanks for the offer though, Charlie. I read about your new menu in the Chronicle. I would love to visit sometime."

"I'll hold you to it, Anna," Charlie Robinson warned. "You ladies have a nice day."

Charlie set off on the Coastal Walk toward the resort. Julie waited until he had put a good distance between them before exploding in anger.

"He's got some gall."

"I thought he was just being polite," Anna said, bewildered.

"Charlie Robinson is a crook," Julie declared. "You better stay away from him, Anna."

"What are you talking about?"

"Don't you know his family's reputation? Smugglers, the lot of them."

"You are being ridiculous!" Anna snapped as they entered the diner. "The locals have always been unkind to the Robinsons."

"There's a reason for that!" Julie cried.

"That's enough," Anna said, holding up a hand. "Weren't you starving?"

"Why don't you order for us?" Julie huffed, folding her hands across her chest.

Anna decided to splurge and ordered root beer floats to go with their double cheeseburgers and fries.

"Do you want your fries crinkle cut?" the waitress asked.

"Of course," Anna nodded.

The crinkle cut fries at the Yellow Tulip were a legend. They were cut by hand and made fresh every day, served with a generous sprinkling of seasoned salt.

"Are you going to stop sulking?" Anna asked Julie after the waitress had left.

"You know Charlie Robinson was flirting with you?"

"You are imagining things, Julie."

"I don't care for that weasel," Julie said unkindly. "But I do think you should start dating. John's been gone for a while."

Anna's eyes welled up.

"I still reach for him in my sleep."

"We know how much you loved him," Julie said softly, patting Anna's hand. "But life has to go on, sweetie. You've still got a couple of decades ahead of you."

"John was looking forward to retirement," Anna shared. "We made big plans. We were going on a Caribbean cruise to celebrate our anniversary. John said it was a dry run for later. He wanted us to go on a world cruise."

Anna swallowed a lump and gave a watery smile when their food arrived. She had suddenly lost her appetite.

"I've spoiled your lunch, haven't I? I'm sorry, Anna."

Anna squirted ketchup over her fries and shook her head.

"I'm always thinking of John, Julie. The truth is, I'm not ready to let him go."

Julie looked contrite as she picked up her burger.

"You know who else was in my class today?"

"Cody," Anna guessed shrewdly.

"How did you know that?" Julie cried. "I was expecting him to come forward and say something about Briana. But he walked out without a word."

"Poor kid," Anna sympathized. "I think he's running scared."

Chapter 19

Anna's mood improved as she gorged on the crispy fries. She decided to snap out of her melancholy mood and focus on the excellent food. Julie kept spouting theories about how someone might be trying to frame Cody.

"Ready for pie?" the waitress came by to ask them.

They agreed to split a slice.

The waitress put in their order for a berry pie and came back to chat with them.

"I heard you talking about that kid Cody," she confessed.

"Do you know him?" Anna asked quickly.

"I sure do," the waitress sighed. "I think he did it. He killed that girl."

"Why do you say that?" Anna cried.

"He's got a short fuse, that one," the waitress said. "He's like a pit bull when he gets angry. And he does that a lot."

"Does he come here?" Julie asked.

"Very often," the waitress nodded. "He came here with that girl. They made a cute couple."

"You think they loved each other?" Anna asked.

"Oh yes," the waitress nodded. "There was no doubt about that. They held hands and whispered to each other, shared their food … they did all the lovey dovey stuff you would expect from a new couple."

"That's a good thing, right?" Anna said. "So there's no doubt Cody loved Briana."

"She seemed more sensible than him," the waitress offered. "This kid used to go off for no reason. She used to talk him down."

"Why was he so angry?" Julie asked.

"I don't know," the waitress shrugged. "It was something different every time."

"What about the girl?" Anna asked. "Did she do anything to set him off?"

"She was a wily one," the waitress said. "Came here with an older man once."

"Would you recognize the man if you saw him again?" Anna asked eagerly.

The waitress shrugged.

"He wasn't a regular. They sat here for a long time, long after I cleared their dinner."

"I'm surprised you remember so much," Julie said. "You must have known the girl well."

"It was because of what happened later," the waitress explained. "I don't know how or why but that kid Cody turned up here. He was fit to be tied."

"You think someone tattled on the girl?" Anna guessed.

"Maybe. The kid grabbed that old man by the collar and lifted him out of that booth like he weighed nothing. He threw him out of the diner and landed a few punches. The older guy's nose was bleeding by the time some people pulled the kid off him."

"That doesn't sound like Cody," Anna muttered.

"You don't believe me?" the waitress challenged. "Ask anyone. A big crowd had gathered outside. People love this kind of drama."

Anna thanked the waitress and asked for their check. She cautioned Julie to stay quiet until they stepped out of the diner.

Her head was whirling with different scenarios on the way back to the store.

Anna and Julie dragged their feet across Ocean Avenue, full from their fast food binge.

"I need a nap," Julie groaned, as they started turning the corner to go over to Main Street.

"Yo Anna!" a voice hailed them.

Jose Garcia waved at them from the other side of a glass window.

"I can't handle this now," Anna muttered, pasting a smile on her face.

Jose beckoned them inside. Anna had no choice but to go in. Julie followed her, looking curious.

"How are you, Jose?" Anna asked wearily.

She looked around her at the cavernous space. It was perfect for her café. The store was empty except for a small folding trestle table at one end and a camp chair. Jose picked up a bunch of photographs that were lying on the table and began showing them to Anna.

"My cousin sent these from Cabo," he said proudly. "This is the pool at his condo, this is the view from the balcony and this is the beach that is a two minute walk away from the condo building. Look at the color of the water, Anna. Look at the bright sunlight. That's where I'm going, Anna."

Anna flipped through the photos and made some appropriate comments. She knew what was coming next.

"You know I can't pass this up, right, Anna?" Jose groveled. "It's my dream retirement."

"You gave me two weeks, Jose," Anna reminded him. "I've still got time."

Jose gave a shrug.

"One week, two weeks, what difference does it make, eh, Anna? You are not getting your license in two weeks."

Julie had finally caught on to what was going on.

"Plenty of people are looking forward to Anna's café," she said. "Anna has a lot of support."

Jose's smile didn't reach his eyes.

"Once you buy the place, you can do what you want with it. Open a café, don't open a café. I'll be soaking up the sun in Cabo."

"He just wants his money, Julie," Anna sighed. "Can't say I blame him."

"That city developer's offer is still open," Jose coaxed. "We both get a big bonus if he can get our two stores. Think about it, Anna. You can get a big payday."

"I'm not selling, Jose," Anna said firmly.

Jose's smile hardened.

"Suit yourself. But your time is running out. I am going to sign the papers as soon as the two weeks are up."

Julie grabbed Anna's arm and stalked out of the store. Anna's hand shook as she tried to insert the key in the lock at the bookstore.

"What's this deadline Jose is talking about?" Julie demanded. "Why haven't you told us about this, Anna?"

"Hey Mom!"

Anna whirled around to see Cassie walking toward the store, holding a paper bag from the Tipsy Whale.

"What are you doing here, child?"

"I came to get some lunch," Cassie said cheerfully. "I got a sandwich for you."

Cassie handed over the bag to her mother.

"We already ate, sweetie," Julie told her. "Why don't you take this home with you?"

Cassie was staring at Anna's face.

"Is something wrong, Mom? You don't look too good."

"I'm fine," Anna snapped. "Just go home, Cassie."

Cassie looked at Julie and raised her eyebrows in question.

"Go on home," Julie said gently. "Your mother just needs a minute."

Cassie looked uncertain as she started walking toward the parking lot. She turned around twice to look at her mother. Anna had finally managed to unlock the door.

Julie sat down on one of the couches with a thud and Anna followed.

Anna looked sad as she talked about the café.

"It was always a pipe dream."

Julie got the story out of Anna.

"Don't worry, Anna," she consoled. "Something will work

out."

"What do you think Briana was doing with that older man?" Anna asked suddenly. "Do you think he was one of her clients?"

Julie thought for a few seconds before shaking her head.

"Remember what we said about those clients? They would want to value their privacy. I don't think one of those creeps would accompany Briana to a public place like that."

"He could have been an uncle," Anna continued. "Or a friend or acquaintance. Why would Cody attack him? You think he suspected Briana of having an affair?"

"Why does everything always come back to Cody?" Julie asked. "You gotta admit, Anna. This kid is either guilty as sin or someone is framing him."

"I'm calling Vicki right now," Anna said. "I want to talk to Cody in her presence. She should be able to spot if he's lying."

"Let's say he is. You think she's going to call him out?"

"If Vicki believes in her son's innocence, she needs to be upfront with us. Cody could be lying for any number of reasons. He could be trying to protect someone. Or he's just afraid."

"You don't want him to be guilty."

"Of course I don't. I've known him since he was a sweet gap toothed kid."

"He's not sweet anymore, judging by what that waitress told us," Julie sighed.

"She made it very clear she doesn't like him," Anna said thoughtfully.

Julie sat up with a jerk, her mouth hanging open.

"I totally forgot something that kid said earlier today."

"You mean that kid from your class?"

Julie nodded urgently.

"Briana got into a fight with another girl."

"When were you planning on telling me that?" Anna exclaimed.

"I barely heard him," Julie admitted grudgingly. "He had been talking for a while and my mind drifted. I just wanted to get out of there and get some coffee."

"Did he say who it was?" Anna asked eagerly.

"He might have, but I don't remember."

"We need to find out who this girl is," Anna said resolutely. "She might tell us more about Briana."

Chapter 20

Cassie sat at the kitchen counter the next morning, drinking her coffee. She had been awake for hours, lying in bed, browsing the tabloids and talking with Bobby on the phone. Her knee was bothering her again and her legs were stiff. Bobby taught her some stretches she could do in bed and talked her into doing them. All Cassie wanted now was to go out to the pool and get some sun.

Anna came out of the room, ready to leave for the store. She looked at Cassie apologetically.

"You'll have to take care of breakfast today, Cassie. I made oatmeal but you don't like it."

Cassie told her not to worry.

"Where are you off to, all dressed up?"

Anna's shoulders slumped.

"Are you going to meet Gino?" Cassie smiled innocently and widened her eyes.

"Now why would I do that?" Anna was indignant.

"Because he's your boyfriend."

"Don't be silly, Cassie. What makes you say that?"

"You like him, don't you? And I'm sure he likes you. He made that very obvious."

"Gino was just being polite," Anna dismissed. "Nothing's going on between us."

Cassie rove her eyes over her mother.

"Isn't that a new top? It's just the right shade of blue. And you're wearing makeup. You haven't done that in months."

"I wanted to look good for a change. Is that a crime?"

"Of course not," Cassie sighed. "I'm happy you are getting back to your old self."

"Can I go now?" Anna scowled.

"Have a nice day, Mom!" Cassie sang. "That scarf's looking awesome, by the way."

Cassie got up to get the box of frosted flakes out of the pantry. She poured a generous helping in a big bowl and added milk. The label on the milk carton announced it was organically produced at the local Daisy Hollow Farm. That made her think of her run-in with Dylan Woods. He had grown into a fine man. She wondered why he wasn't married yet.

Cassie flicked the channels on the TV for some time, stopping when she came across a rival actress on a talk show. It had been a while since Cassie had been on any shows. She made some choice comments at the screen and then tossed the remote over a chair.

A nap seemed appealing and Cassie dozed off with the TV blaring in the background. She woke up an hour later, itching to do something. The brochures from Dolphin Bay University lay scattered on the coffee table. Cassie decided to go enroll in a class.

Dolphin Bay University was a hive of activity. The admissions office was housed in a separate building next to the library. The lady in charge frowned when she learnt Cassie hadn't finished high school.

"We don't have many options for dropouts," she grimaced. "You at least need a GED."

Cassie didn't take it to heart. She knew some of her achievements were much bigger than a college degree.

"I just want to occupy myself," she told the woman. "What about the courses at the culinary school?"

"You will get a certificate," the woman informed her. "But no college credits, okay? If you want to do a degree at some later point, you will have to start from scratch."

Cassie took a stack of application forms and walked out, promising to turn them in before the end of the week. A cluster of students was gathered outside the library. Cassie recognized the girl in the big blown up photo. Flowers and candles were placed below it, along with teddy bears and cards. It was a memorial for Briana Parks.

Cassie went and stood there with the students, trying to listen in on what they were saying. The crowd dwindled until only one girl remained. She sat cross legged on the floor, clutching a bunch of wildflowers. Tears streamed down her cheeks and fell on her T-shirt.

Cassie didn't hesitate. She sat on the ground next to the girl and placed a hand on her back.

"Did you know her well?"

"Briana was my friend," the girl said miserably. "I can't believe she's gone."

That brought a fresh onslaught of tears.

"I'm Cassie."

"Sherrie," the girl mumbled through her tears.

"Looks like she was very popular around here."

"Briana was so smart," the girl called Sherrie said. "Everyone envied her."

"I heard some girls talking about her," Cassie admitted. "I think they were just being catty."

"Briana was super ambitious," Sherrie disclosed. "That didn't go down too well with some of the kids."

"What's wrong with being ambitious?" Cassie wondered. "Isn't that why kids come to college? To build a good future?"

"You would think so," the girl sighed. "Most kids are just interested in going to parties and getting drunk."

"So Briana wasn't a party girl?"

Sherrie shook her head.

"She just liked to show off. She acted like she came from a rich family so the kids expected her to throw some money around."

"And she didn't do that."

"No," Sherrie said. "Briana could barely pay the fees when she first got here."

She hesitated.

"Go on," Cassie said encouragingly. "Did she hit the lottery or something?"

"Briana got a job," Sherri said. "It paid well. She had something left over after paying the fees. She started spending it on herself. Bought new clothes. Then she got that new car."

"What did she do?" Cassie asked, wide eyed. "Sell an arm and a leg?"

Sherrie dried her eyes with her shirt. She looked over her shoulder and sidled closer to Cassie.

"It was a bit unconventional."

Cassie summoned all her acting skills and maintained a poker face.

"I don't believe in judging people. I've had to do some twisted things to get ahead in life."

Sherrie leaned toward Cassie and gushed.

"Briana worked as a hired date."

"You mean like an escort?"

"Not really. More of a stand-in. It was all above board, you know. No hanky panky. Most of the guys she went out with were older men. They just needed the company."

"How did she get into all this? Was it through some website?"

"It's mostly word of mouth," Sherrie said. "These men value their privacy. They are not ready to post their profiles online."

"You seem to know a lot about it."

Sherrie looked over her shoulder again.

"Actually, it's kind of my thing. I found a need and decided to fill it. I vet all the girls and fix the appointments. There are strict rules. They can't tell anyone about it, not even their boyfriends. And pictures are forbidden. They can't post photos on social."

"How do you get paid?" Cassie asked.

"I take a percentage off the top. Payments are in cash only. Everyone is happy."

"Have you been on one of these dates?" Cassie was curious.

Sherrie pointed at her thick horn rimmed glasses and skinny five foot frame.

"Me?" she laughed. "My girls are hot! Who's going to pay to take a plain girl out on a date?"

"What if someone misbehaves?"

"Then the girls are on their own," Sherrie shrugged. "They know there's an element of risk here. They do it for the money."

"Did Briana have a problem with any of her clients?"

"Not as far as I know. Why?"

"What if she got into a fight with her date? You think that man might have harmed her?"

"I don't think so," Sherrie said stoutly. "Briana's boyfriend is the guilty one. I hear the police have clear evidence against him."

"How can you say for sure? She might have been on a date on the night she died."

Sherrie nodded.

"I completely forgot about that. I think she was supposed to go out that night."

"Do you know who with?"

Sherrie pulled out a small diary from her messenger bag and flipped through the pages. She jabbed her finger at an entry.

"It's right here. She was meeting Doug Crane. He's a Silicon Valley geek. There was a big technology conference here that day and he needed a plus one."

"Did Briana keep her appointment?"

"I don't know," Sherrie said. "I don't keep tabs on them. Briana usually got back to me in a day or two with my commission. But she was gone by that time."

A fresh burst of tears spilled from Sherrie's eyes. Cassie took her arm in hers and tried to pacify the girl.

"I don't trust that Cody at all," Sherrie cried suddenly. "I'm pretty sure he did it."

Cassie bit back a groan and started talking to the girl about Cody.

Chapter 21

A bank of clouds had crept up over the bay by the time Cassie got home. She had accompanied Sherrie to the university cafeteria for lunch. Cassie had been dismayed when Sherrie thanked her for lending a kind ear.

"Just like my Mom! I miss her a lot, you know. But my family's back east and I rarely get to see them."

Cassie wondered if she was looking that frumpy. Since a spa wasn't a part of Cassie's budget, she decided to do some DIY. She slathered a mask on her face and neck, placed cucumber slices on her eyes and went to sleep.

The sky had darkened when Cassie woke up from her nap. She admired the riot of colors the setting sun had painted on the horizon. Her stomach rumbled, signaling it was time to make dinner.

Cassie had very few dishes in her repertoire. Chicken Fried Rice and Cobb Salad with the Goddess dressing were her specialty. She chose the salad and hoped her mother wouldn't make a fuss.

"Salad again?" Anna grumbled when they sat down for dinner. "You need to learn how to cook a proper meal."

"This salad has all the food groups, Mom," Cassie said patiently. "And I made my special dressing."

"I do love that Goddess dressing," Anna said, slightly mollified.

She took a big bite of the salad and smiled appreciatively.

"Watch any new movies?" she asked Cassie.

"I don't sit around watching TV all day, Mom," Cassie said drily. "I went to the college and spoke to the admissions coordinator."

"Really?" Anna asked. "Are you signing up for that health food course then?"

Cassie told her about the admission forms. Anna offered to help fill them out.

"Did anyone talk about John?"

"I don't think they knew I was his daughter, Mom."

"Your father loved teaching," Anna reminisced. "They made him an Emeritus professor, you know. He was so proud about it."

"Dad died too soon," Cassie said, swallowing a lump in her throat. "I never thought I wouldn't get to spend time with him again."

"Life's fickle, kiddo. Remember that. You never know what's around the next corner."

"Speaking of ..." Cassie began. "There was some kind of shrine for Briana at the college."

"Was Cody there?"

"No, he wasn't. But I met Sherrie."

"Sherrie? You mean the girl who Briana was working for?" Anna asked excitedly.

"The very same," Cassie told her. "We got talking."

"Did you learn anything new?"

"Did I?" Cassie laughed. "Sherrie's a young slip of a girl. Wears thick glasses. You would never know how enterprising she was by looking at her."

Cassie told Anna about Sherrie's business model.

"She didn't think it was immoral?"

"I don't think so. As far as she is concerned, the girls were just going out on a date."

Anna grunted in disapproval.

"Sherrie believes Cody is guilty."

"What's he done to her?"

"He did plenty to Briana, according to Sherrie. Briana was sick of him. She wanted to break up. But Cody wouldn't let her go."

"Go on."

"They got into a big fight. I think Cody must have threatened Briana or attacked her. Sherrie's not sure exactly what happened. But Briana called the police."

"Did the police arrest Cody?" Anna asked, alert. "Why has no one mentioned this before?"

"Apparently, the police just counseled them. They let Cody go with a warning. No complaint was registered."

"Even if there is no record of this incident, the policemen involved will remember," Anna mused. "And they talk amongst each other, just like anyone else."

"Do you think that's the reason the police have been set against Cody since the beginning?" Cassie wondered. "He's already proved he can be violent."

"I think the fingerprints are more damning than this incident. But something like this can just add fuel to the fire."

Cassie got up to clear the plates.

"We are skipping dessert today, Mom."

"No way," Anna said, scandalized. "There's a pint of chocolate gelato in the freezer."

"No, there isn't. I ate it."

"Julie always stocks plenty of ice cream. I'm going to call her."

Cassie burst out laughing.

"Relax, Mom. I got a pie from the market earlier. And

vanilla ice cream."

Anna glared at her daughter.

"I don't see what's funny."

Cassie took the pie out of the refrigerator and cut two generous slices. She warmed them up in the microwave and scooped some vanilla ice cream on top of each slice.

"Oh, I almost forgot. Sherrie had an appointment diary. Briana was supposed to meet a guy that day."

"Does she know this guy?" Anna asked sharply.

"She had a name. She wasn't sure if Briana actually kept the appointment."

"We need to track this guy down, Cassie. He can tell us about the last day of Briana's life."

"He might have been the last person to see her alive, Mom."

"Last, or last but one."

"I wonder if the police know about this guy. He seems like a suspect to me."

"You think he could have hurt Briana?" Anna asked.

"What do we really know about him, Mom? Sherrie said he's some techie from the Valley. He could be a psycho for all we know."

"That's farfetched."

"If he actually met Briana, it's not," Cassie argued.

"What about that girl you met? Sherrie? How do you know she didn't have it in for Briana?"

"Sherrie seemed like a nice girl."

"Appearances are deceptive, Cassie. I don't understand one thing. How come she let you ask so many questions?"

"Sherrie was very distressed when I ran into her. I think she just needed a shoulder to cry on."

"Looks like she trusted you."

Cassie rolled her eyes.

"She thought I was some kind of mother figure. Do I look that old?"

"I'm not answering that question. But you are old enough to be her mother."

"I'm going to go online and try to get some info on Doug Crane."

"Is that the techie guy?"

Cassie nodded.

"I need a favor," Anna said. "Can you open the bookstore tomorrow morning? I have to go meet Vicki Bauer."

"I was planning to sleep in tomorrow," Cassie groaned. "I've had a hectic day today, Mom."

"Never mind," Anna muttered. "I shouldn't have asked."

"What if we open a couple of hours late?" Cassie asked.

"I've been running Bayside Books for twenty years, Cassie. I always open at a certain time. People expect it."

"Okay, okay," Cassie sighed. "I'll do it."

"Try not to make a mess like you did last time," Anna warned. "Once you open the store, you need to dust all the shelves."

Cassie listened glumly as her mother outlined a bunch of chores she needed to do.

"Did you meet that girl who's living at Aunt Mary's?" Cassie asked.

Anna slapped her forehead. "I forgot all about her."

"You don't seriously suspect her, do you?"

"I don't know if I told you," Anna said. "Mary found Briana's contact information in her things."

"You should ask Cody about her."

"Good idea," Anna said. "I'll make a note of that."

"Do you know anything about the Castle Beach Resort, Mom?"

"Funny you should ask. I ran into Charlie Robinson earlier today. He wanted me to try out the food at his restaurant."

"You don't mean Dad's old friend? I remember he used to get candy for me every time he came home to see Dad."

"The same," Anna nodded. "Although he and your Dad weren't talking to each other."

"Why is he asking you to lunch?" Cassie asked slyly. "Don't tell me you have one more admirer."

Anna turned red.

"Don't be ridiculous. I've barely said a word to him in the past decade."

"What about this resort, though? Bobby's thinking of getting a room there when he comes to visit."

"It's very expensive."

"That won't matter to Bobby. He's loaded."

"Why does he want to go to a hotel? I thought you knew him well."

"He's my bestie," Cassie nodded. "Bobby's stuck with me through a lot of bad times."

"Then why aren't you inviting him here? We have a couple of spare rooms."

"Are you serious, Mom?" Cassie's eyes lit up.

"We are not as fancy as the resort …"

"That's awesome, Mom!" Cassie cried, leaping across the table to give Anna a hug. "Bobby asked to come stay here but I wasn't sure."

"Why not? This is your home, sweetie, such as it is. You don't need my permission to invite anyone."

Cassie's eyes were moist with tears as she gazed lovingly at her mother.

"Thanks for making me feel so welcome, Mom."

Chapter 22

Anna fixed herself an extra cup of coffee the next morning. She wanted to be alert when she met Vicki and Cody. She knocked on Cassie's door to wake her up.

There was a muffled groan from the other side.

Anna fixed avocado toast for the both of them and rushed through her own breakfast. She was relieved to see Cassie enter the kitchen, all showered and dressed.

"Good Morning, Mom." Cassie yawned. "When are you meeting your friend?"

"As soon as I get there," Anna quipped.

"Do you need a ride?"

Anna hesitated.

Vicki Bauer lived about a mile away on top of a small hill. Anna remembered how her legs had protested when she went to the winery.

"Don't bother. I think I can manage it."

"You can always call Gino to pick you up," Cassie joked.

Anna ignored her and wound a scarf around her shoulders. She wore a broad hat that would protect her from the sun.

She straddled her bike and started pedaling toward Vicki's house.

Vicki opened the door, looking red and blotchy.

"Have you been crying?" Anna asked with concern.

"We just heard from the lawyer. The police might be making an arrest today."

Anna bit back her response. She was surprised the police had held off for so long. They must be waiting on some reports.

"Everything will be fine, Vicki," she consoled. "Why don't you sit down and take a breath? Let me get you some tea."

Anna rooted around in the cabinets and found a pack of chamomile. She brewed the tea, added some honey and urged Vicki to drink it.

"This will calm you down."

"Have you made any progress, Anna?" Vicki asked earnestly. "Do you think you can help Cody?"

Anna considered a diplomatic reply.

"Give it to me straight," Vicki sighed. "We will have to face the truth some time."

"Things don't look good for Cody," Anna admitted. "Almost every person I talked to thinks he is guilty. His temper is infamous, Vicki. People have seen him getting into fights. That doesn't look good."

"Cody used to be so easy-going," Vicki reminisced. "He changed when he injured that elbow. He lost his scholarship and his dreams shattered overnight."

"That was a while ago," Anna reasoned. "It's no excuse for flinging his fists around now."

"I don't know how to handle him," Vicki sobbed. "He's staying out late at night. I think he's been drinking."

"Cody hasn't been completely honest with me. I think he's hiding something."

Vicki's expression hardened. She got up and went inside. Anna heard her banging on a door. Anna remembered Vicki couldn't afford college housing so Cody still lived at home.

Anna heard a muted conversation and Vicki came back.

"He'll be out in a minute."

Cody stepped into the living room right after, wearing a crumpled shirt that looked like it came out of the laundry basket. His eyes were bloodshot and the expression on his face was grumpy.

"Anna has some questions for you, Cody. Make sure you tell her everything. Don't leave anything out."

Anna observed Cody from the corner of her eye. She decided he was definitely hung over. She wasn't impressed.

Cody let out a wide yawn.

"I stand by what I said, Mrs. Butler. I was in love with Briana. I would never hurt her."

"That's not going to be good enough, Cody," Anna told him. "We need to prove you did not hurt that girl. Now try to answer my questions as honestly and completely as you can. Don't leave anything out. The smallest detail might be important."

Cody sat forward in his chair and gave Anna a nod.

"Based on the autopsy report, Briana died sometime between 4 PM and 7 PM. Where were you at that time?"

"I was driving to the college to pick Briana up," Cody said. "We had a date that night."

"So you met her?" Anna asked with bated breath.

"No," Cody shook his head. "She wasn't where she was supposed to be. I waited for almost half an hour, hoping she would turn up. Then I got mad and drove off."

"What about the baseball bat? How does it have your prints on it?"

Cody looked flustered.

"It does belong to me," he admitted.

"What?" Vicki cried. "You never told me that."

"I didn't want to worry you, Mom," Cody explained. He looked at Anna. "I lent it to Briana. Their class had a student versus teachers game coming up."

"Did you tell this to the police?" Anna asked.

"They just wanted to know if the bat belonged to me."

"You are being too casual about this," Anna grumbled. "No wonder people think you did it."

Cody excused himself for a minute and went inside. He came back with a glass of orange juice.

"What was this scuffle you got into with Briana?" Anna inquired. "Did you hit her or not?"

Vicki let out another cry.

"Did you hit a woman, Cody? Surely I raised you better than that?"

Cody looked guilty.

"I didn't beat her, Mom. But I came close. Look, I am ashamed of it, okay?"

"Tell us what happened," Anna prompted.

"We had a big argument. I don't remember much of it. I must have threatened Briana. She called the cops."

"I heard they didn't register a complaint against you?" Anna asked. "What did the cops say?"

"Actually, I lost all my bluster as soon as the police arrived. I couldn't believe Briana called them. They talked to us for a while. I assured them I had no intention of harming my girl. They must have believed me because they left soon after."

Anna observed Cody as he sat there, wringing his hands in despair. She wasn't convinced of his innocence.

"What about Briana's friends?" Anna asked. "Can you think of anyone who might have wanted to harm her?"

Cody's face darkened. He cleared his throat and hesitated.

"Don't keep anything back, Cody," Anna urged. "Your future is on the line here."

"Are you trying to protect someone?" Vicki wailed.

Cody expelled a breath and nodded at his mother.

"Briana was having an affair."

"What!" Anna and Vicki exclaimed at the same time.

"She was cheating on me, Mom!" Cody sounded anguished. "I called her out on it but she wouldn't admit it. We argued about it a lot."

"What made you suspect her?" Anna asked.

"I don't know," Cody shrugged. "Call it gut instinct. I tried to find proof. I went through her stuff, checked her emails and texts. But I couldn't find anything."

"You mean you spied on her?" Anna asked.

No wonder Briana wanted to break up, Anna thought. But she didn't say anything out loud.

"I had no choice," Cody said, looking miserable. "I'm sure it was someone at the college. But Briana wouldn't own up to it. I told her I was ready to forgive her. She just needed to tell me the truth."

"I don't think this girl was good for you," Vicki said, sounding like a protective mother hen.

"That's a moot point now, Vicki," Anna reminded her.

She turned toward Cody and chose her words carefully.

"There is something you don't know."

She told him about the work Briana did as a stand-in. Vicki was aghast. Cody looked surprised.

"So she just had to go out on a date, right? She didn't need to get involved with these people."

Anna nodded. "It was just part of her job. I'm sure she didn't actually care for these people."

Cody didn't look convinced.

"She was seeing someone apart from these people then. I'm sure of it."

"It doesn't make sense at the moment," Anna shared. "But I will look into this. I promise."

"How can I thank you enough, Anna?" Vicki sobbed, dabbing her eyes with a tissue.

"Come to book club," Anna joked.

"When are you opening that café, Anna?" Vicki asked.

"I hit a snag. Doesn't look like I am going to open that café."

"You're a strong woman, Anna. Don't give up so soon."

Anna squared her shoulders and gave Vicki a wan smile.

"Some obstacles are insurmountable."

"I heard the rumors that are flying around," Vicki said softly. "I don't believe them one bit."

Anna shrugged and said nothing.

"You've got a lot of people rooting for you, Anna."

"Thank you, Vicki. Mary's got some kind of petition going. Why don't you check it out?"

Vicki promised to get in touch with Mary. Anna said goodbye to mother and son and started cycling to the bookstore. She thought over the new information she had learned. If Cody was right about Briana's affair, he had one more reason to harm her.

Was Briana really in love with someone else?

Chapter 23

The spring day was bright and sunny and Anna decided to take the scenic route back to the store. She rode over to her favorite bench on the Coastal Walk. It offered a great view of the cliffs and the sea. Poppies nodded in the breeze, carpeting the bluffs in a blaze of orange. A couple of dolphins frolicked in the water in the distance.

People were out for a walk, enjoying the fine day. Some of them waved at Anna. Some went out of their way to avoid her. Anna squared her shoulders and stood up to leave.

Bayside Books was doing brisk business when Anna went back. She sat in an armchair and played the part of a silent observer. Cassie was chatting with the customers gaily, urging them to come back soon. The store emptied after a while. Cassie's phone rang and she paced the floor, talking to someone earnestly about a role.

Anna hailed her daughter after she hung up.

"Mom! When did you get back?"

"A few minutes ago," Anna replied. "Was that your agent?"

Cassie nodded.

"Did you just turn down an offer for work?"

"It was just a cameo, Mom. Not the kind of comeback I am

looking for."

"I don't understand you, Cassie. I thought you needed the money."

"It's complicated, okay? You won't understand, Mom."

Anna went into the pantry, muttering to herself. She hoped Cassie wasn't throwing away a good opportunity just to stay in Dolphin Bay and look after her.

"I am recovering well, Cassie," she said. "I'm strong enough to take care of myself."

"Of course you are. How did it go with Cody?"

Anna gave Cassie a brief account of what she had learnt.

"This is the first we are hearing of Briana's affair. Do you think it was one of her clients?"

"I don't know. I am going to meet the Firecrackers for lunch. Do you have any plans?"

"I thought I would go and turn in those admission forms."

Anna told Cassie to grab an early lunch. She forced herself to do some paperwork for the next hour, waiting for the town clock to signal it was noon. Flipping the door sign to Closed, Anna locked up the store and walked to the Tipsy Whale.

Julie and Mary had already grabbed a booth.

"We are ordering today's special," Julie informed Anna.

"Pulled pork sandwiches with a side of fries. Shall I get the same for you?"

Anna's mouth watered.

"Sounds yum. But I'll take onion rings instead of the fries."

Anna admired some pictures of Mary's grandkids while Julie ordered their food. The waitress brought over tall glasses of sweet tea.

"How was your meeting with Vicki and that kid?" Mary asked.

Anna voiced her concerns.

"He's taking it hard, poor boy. But I still can't say I trust him completely."

"Wait till you hear what I found," Julie stepped in.

Anna waited impatiently while she took a deep sip of her drink.

"Briana was having an affair."

She sat back with a knowing smile and twitched her eyebrows at Anna.

"That's what Cody thought!" Anna exclaimed. "How did you find out, Julie?"

"I have a new neighbor," Julie began. "I knew someone had moved into the little house next door but I wasn't really paying attention. The owner rents it out over the

Internet, I think. There's always someone moving in or moving out."

"Julie! Get to the point."

"You remember how Charlie Robinson wanted you to taste the new menu at his restaurant?"

"What does that have to do with anything?" Anna asked, bewildered.

"My new neighbor is the celebrated chef he was talking about."

"Your neighbor is the new fancy chef at the Castle Beach Resort?" Mary prompted. "Make nice with him, Julie. He might let us taste his food."

"Anna's already making nice with Charlie Robinson," Julie chortled. "We have an open invitation to the restaurant."

"Girls!" Anna cried. "Stop straying from the topic. Tell me what he said, Julie."

"Briana visited the resort restaurant often, with an older man."

"How does this chef know Briana?" Anna asked.

"He saw her picture in the Chronicle."

"Why hasn't he come forward with this information?"

"No one asked him, I guess. It's not against the law to have dinner with someone."

"Why did he tell you all this?" Mary wondered.

"He's a big gossip, that's why," Julie smirked.

Anna reminded them about the work Briana did for Sherrie.

"How do we know this old man wasn't just one of her clients?" Anna mused.

"That's hard to say," Julie agreed. "Do you think Briana might have confided in someone about this man?"

"Cody guessed Briana was seeing someone else. She denied it."

"Could this man have hurt Briana?" Mary asked timidly.

"We do have one more potential suspect," Julie agreed. "This is good for Cody."

"Is it?" Anna asked. "What if he was mad at Briana for cheating on him?"

"Well, if you put it that way..." Julie shrugged.

Their food arrived and they shifted their attention to the steaming sandwiches.

"Murphy makes the best barbecue sauce," Julie said, licking her fingers. "I've been trying to convince him to bottle it."

"He can sell some at the farmer's market," Mary said.

"We need to find out more about this older man," Anna

said, picking up a fry from Mary's plate. "He might tell us more about Briana."

"Not if their affair was supposed to be secret. He'll try to deny any involvement with Briana."

The group dispersed after lunch. Mary had to rush to a dentist's appointment. Julie walked back to the store with Anna.

"How's your latest book coming?" Anna asked her.

"I'm half way through. But I'm stuck. I need to clear my mind completely."

"You can help me catalog all these new books," Anna said, pointing to a big box of books that had been delivered that morning.

"I didn't say I want to be put to work," Julie pouted.

The doorbell jangled just then and a young dark haired man came in. He was dressed casually in a polo shirt and chinos. He pulled a slip of paper out of his pocket and headed straight toward Anna.

"I'm looking for a book," he mumbled.

"Why don't you give me that?" Anna held out her hand for the piece of paper.

She read the title and looked apologetic.

"We don't stock a lot of technical books. But let me check my catalog, just in case."

She tapped a few keys on the computer and searched her inventory.

"Sorry. We don't have it."

The man didn't leave right away. His face had reddened a bit.

"Can I help you with something else?" Anna asked kindly.

Julie watched the man with narrowed eyes.

"Are you Cassie?" he asked.

Anna's face cleared.

"Cassie's my daughter," she replied. "She's not here right now."

"I can wait," the man said meekly.

"I'm not sure if she's coming back to the store today," Anna supplied. "Do you know her from L.A.?"

"I don't know her at all," the man said.

Anna stared at him blankly. She had no idea what was going on.

"My name is Doug Crane."

"Where have I heard that name recently?"

"You're not from around here, are you?" Julie asked.

"I live in Silicon Valley."

"Now I remember!" Anna opened her mouth and paused. "You are one of Sherrie's guys, aren't you?"

The man nodded miserably.

"I don't know how your daughter got my number. I have a very small digital presence. I pay people big money to keep my contact information private."

Anna knew her daughter was no techno geek.

"Does Sherrie have your number?" she asked.

"I guess so."

"That's how Cassie tracked you down."

"Can someone tell me what's going on?" Julie demanded. "Who is this guy?"

"You know the dating business Sherrie runs? Doug here was supposed to go out with Briana the day she died."

Julie's eyes widened as she gave the young man a once over.

"Why does a young man like you need a hired date? Can't you get a girl on your own?"

Doug looked embarrassed.

"I was here for a big tech conference. They changed the invitations after I got here. Where was I supposed to get a plus one at the last minute?"

"Never mind all that," Anna soothed. She gave Julie a warning look. "Did you meet Briana that evening?"

Doug nodded.

"I picked her up at the given address."

"How long was she with you?" Anna asked with bated breath.

"Barely ten minutes," Doug Crane replied. "She was very distracted when I picked her up. We were on our way to the conference when she suddenly demanded I stop the car."

"Do you remember where that was?"

"Not really. I am new to this area."

"Was it somewhere near the redwood forest?" Anna asked.

"The whole area we were driving through seemed wooded."

"What did you do then?"

"I pulled over," Doug said. "She got out and started walking away without a backward glance."

"Did she say where she was going, or why?"

"No explanations," Doug said with a shake of his head. "I waited for a few minutes, thinking she might come back. Then I had to drive off."

"How do we know you are telling the truth?" Anna asked.

"Dozens of people saw me at that conference," Doug Crane told them. "Why would I want to hurt her? I barely knew her."

"Thanks for coming here, Doug. If you are really innocent, you won't mind repeating all this to the police?"

"That's where I am going next."

Chapter 24

Cassie had taken Anna's advice. She stood in line at the Tipsy Whale, salivating at the sweet, smoky aromas that swirled around her.

"One Special of the Day with extra coleslaw," she told Murphy. "My Mom's coming here too. She'll be here soon."

Murphy grunted and rang up her purchase. Cassie was in a chatty mood. She asked Murphy if he posted his menu online. Murphy told her he didn't have a website. He wasn't going to have one. He had been writing the day's special on a chalkboard out on the sidewalk for thirty five years. He would continue doing so until he ran the pub.

"Your city ways won't fly here," a deep voice said.

Cassie whirled around to stare at the tall, brown eyed man standing in line behind her.

"Dylan."

"Cassie. Are you done? Some of us have work to get back to."

Cassie moved aside from the counter. She opened her mouth to say something smart and acerbic but nothing came to mind.

"We get your milk," she said instead. "I saw your name on the carton."

"Anna was one of the first to try our organic line. She's always been a strong advocate of Daisy Hollow Farms."

Dylan placed his order and leaned against the wooden counter, his hands in his pockets.

"It's a beautiful day," Cassie noted. "Nice day to sit on a park bench and enjoy lunch."

"I have to get back to the farm, Cassie."

Cassie turned red.

"I wasn't … I didn't mean …"

Dylan Woods flashed a cocky grin as he picked up his sandwich bag.

"I know!"

Cassie watched his back as he breezed out of the door, feeling like a fool. She crept out with her cheeks flaming, hoping no one had heard her talking to Dylan. There was a small park a few doors down from the pub, right in the middle of Main Street. It housed a gazebo which was the pride of downtown Dolphin Bay. Smarting from Dylan's snub, Cassie decided she was going to enjoy her pulled pork sandwich at the gazebo. She admired the pink and purple wisteria hanging down the gazebo. Climbing roses wound around the pillars, perfuming the air with their heady scent.

Cassie's mood improved by the time she finished her lunch.

A nap was calling her name but she persevered. Deciding it was now or never, she walked to the parking lot and got into her car, determined to turn in the admission forms.

Dolphin Bay University was the usual beehive of activity. The woman at the admissions office greeted her like an old friend.

"You made a good choice," she said. "If you get your GED, these health food courses can count toward a nutrition degree."

"Thanks. But I'm not sure I'm cut out for that."

The woman looked disappointed. Cassie wondered if she got a commission for getting students to enroll in certain courses. She walked out of the building, wondering where she could find Sherrie. Was she also an English major like Briana?

A lot of students were outdoors, taking advantage of the fine day. Some reclined under trees with their nose in a book. Others sat around in groups, engrossed in lively discussions. Cassie decided to tackle the library first. She spotted an empty bench outside and sat down, observing the kids as they streamed in or out. Her patience was rewarded some time later.

Sherrie walked out of the library, a heavy satchel slung over her shoulders. She was typing something on her phone with her head down, eyes glued to the screen. She didn't see Cassie waving at her.

"Sherrie. Over here. Sherrie!"

Sherrie finally looked up. Her face broke into a smile. She rushed to envelop Cassie in a hug.

"This is a surprise."

"I had to submit some documents," Cassie explained. "I was hoping to run into you."

Sherrie's face fell.

"Has your mother made any progress?"

"This might not be news to you. Briana was cheating on Cody."

Sherrie's shoulders slumped.

"It was bound to come out sooner or later."

"You knew?" Cassie's eyes widened.

"I had a hunch. Briana had a huge crush on this guy. She used to get all worked up when she was going to meet him. I called her out on it but she denied it."

"Who was he?"

Sherrie leaned forward and dropped her voice a notch.

"Her English professor. He was kind of a mentor to her in the beginning. He took her under his wing, gave her special attention."

"Is he just out of college himself?"

"Oh no. He's much older, old enough to be her father."

"Was he forcing her, do you think? Misusing his power?"

Sherrie was thoughtful.

"I'm not sure. Far as I can tell, Briana hero worshipped him. She just couldn't stop talking about how smart he was."

"How did she meet him?"

"He's one of the top professors in the department. His class is really hard to get into and harder to pass. But once you get in, you learn a lot."

"Did you take that class too?"

"Last semester," Sherrie sighed. "I was the one who pushed Briana into taking that class. She dreamed of being a news anchor one day. This class would help get her there."

"So this professor guy ... does he prey on the girls a lot? I mean, is he a habitual offender?"

Sherrie denied hearing any such rumors about the man.

"Do you think the professor might have hurt Briana?" Sherrie asked, her eyes filling with horror.

"I don't know, Sherrie. I'm just learning about him."

"It's all my fault. I pushed Briana toward him."

Sherrie's eyes filled with tears.

"You are not to blame," Cassie said firmly. "You couldn't

know she would fall for this granddad."

Sherrie remembered she had a class to go to. She wiped her eyes, thanked Cassie and walked away. Cassie's knees creaked as she stood up to leave. She decided to stretch her legs a bit before heading home.

Cassie spotted the coffee cart just when she was beginning to long for a hot drink. She ordered a nonfat mocha with extra whipped cream and waited for the barista to fill her order. A head of bright blue grabbed her attention and Cassie smiled when she recognized the petite figure striding toward her.

"Hello! You're still here."

"Yes, I am," the girl laughed. "Sat through a drama class today. It was fun."

"They let you do that?"

"Most of them don't mind. Some don't even realize I am an outsider."

"So you like our little town, huh?"

"I really do. It's pretty out here. And quiet. I could get used to it."

"Are you still living at Aunt Mary's?"

The girl called Rain pursed her lips.

"I don't know how much longer I can afford it, though. I need to find a job."

"What kind of job?"

"I'm not picky. Anything that pays the bills."

"Why don't you come and work for my mother?"

Rain's eyes lit up.

"Is she hiring?"

"We can always use some help. It's a bookstore. Bayside Books. On the corner of Main and Ocean."

"I know where it is."

"Fantastic!"

"Thank you so much," Rain gushed. "You have saved me a lot of trouble."

"I'm just doing myself a favor. My Mom won't keep flooding me with chores if she has some help."

"I won't let you down. I promise."

"You know, I was a lot like you when I was younger."

Rain's interest was genuine.

"Did you also travel across the country?"

"Hardly," Cassie laughed. "I went south and stopped in Los Angeles. But that's exactly where I wanted to be."

"What's special about Los Angeles?" Rain asked innocently.

"Hollywood, of course. I dreamed of being in the movies ever since I was a little girl. I wanted to be a famous actress, like Meg Ryan."

"Isn't she old?"

"This was twenty years ago. Meg Ryan was a top star at that time."

"Did you do it?" Rain asked curiously. "Did you become famous?"

"I guess I did," Cassie sighed. "I have a star on the Hollywood Walk of Fame."

Rain had never heard of it.

"I won an Oscar at 21."

Rain had heard of the Oscar award. She was suitably impressed.

"You must be smart!"

Cassie had a faraway look in her eyes.

"I had ambition. Plenty of it. I worked hard and I was fortunate to get the right breaks."

"Doesn't hurt that you look gorgeous."

"It came with a price, of course. I made big sacrifices."

"I'm not ambitious at all," Rain said lightly. "I take life one day at a time."

"You are fearless," Cassie noted. "You meet life head on. Mark my words, sweetie. It will take you far."

A light blush spread across the girl's cheeks.

"I have to go now. It's been nice talking to you."

Cassie sipped her coffee and stared at Rain's retreating back. She wondered why she felt so drawn to her.

Chapter 25

The sun had set by the time Cassie woke from her nap. She had been exhausted by all the walking she had done on the campus. An aroma of roasted garlic filled the house. Cassie dragged herself into the kitchen and pulled up a chair.

"Something smells good. What are you cooking, Mom?"

Anna picked up the mound of fresh cut vegetables and added them to a pot.

"Pasta Prima Vera. I got some nice fresh asparagus and peas at the farm."

"Sounds great. I'm starving."

Anna pulled out a pan of crostini from the oven. She spooned different toppings on them and offered them to Cassie.

"We can start with the bruschetta. Why don't you pour the wine?"

"I had the best day," Cassie enthused. "Time goes by really fast at the university."

Anna hummed a tune as she whisked a creamy sauce. She added a few handfuls of shredded cheese from the piles she had ready on a cutting board. Cassie was glad to see her in a good mood.

"Looks like you had a great day too, Mom."

"I had a busy day. I am happy when I am working."

Cassie gobbled the bruschetta and waited eagerly for Anna to finish tossing the pasta together. Anna served the pasta in bright blue stoneware bowls, topped them with extra virgin olive oil and grated parmesan cheese and placed one before Cassie.

"I ran into Sherrie again," Cassie said, scooping up a big forkful of the rich, creamy pasta. "She told me Briana was mad about one of her professors."

"Was he an older guy?" Anna asked.

"How did you know?" Cassie's mouth dropped open in amazement.

"We need to swap notes. Julie got talking to one of her neighbors. It seems Briana visited Castle Beach Resort very often. She has been seen with an older man."

"Sherrie wasn't sure if Briana was just throwing herself on him. But looks like he was involved too."

"How do we know it wasn't platonic? Maybe he was just being kind to her."

"Or he was taking unfair advantage of his position," Cassie pointed out.

"Poor Cody. Looks like he might have been right about Briana."

Cassie took a second helping of the pasta and offered the rest to her mother.

"We need to find out more about this professor."

"Your father would have known," Anna said. "He had a wide social circle."

"Can't you ask Aunt Julie?" Cassie prompted. "She might have some contacts in the English department."

"Wonderful idea. I will call her as soon as we finish eating."

"Are we having tiramisu for dessert?" Cassie asked.

"Not tonight. I made some amaretto cookies. We can have them with lemon gelato."

"I met that girl who's living at Aunt Mary's."

Anna's eyes widened.

"I forgot all about her. She's a suspect too. She had Briana's contact info among her things."

"I don't think Rain had anything to do with Briana. She's a sweet kid."

"You barely know her."

"I offered her a job at the store, Mom."

"What!" Anna exclaimed. "We can't afford to hire anyone. The store barely breaks even."

"You can use the help," Cassie argued. "You have to stop

climbing up on that ladder, anyway. She can do the heavy lifting."

"You should have asked me first, Cassie."

"You won't have to close the store when you step out for lunch," Cassie pointed out. "And you won't have to call me over."

"What brought this on?"

"She needs rent money," Cassie explained. "She said she was willing to do any job."

"I'll try her out for a couple of weeks."

"She can help you with the petition," Cassie said suddenly. "She can go door to door and get signatures for us."

"I don't think the good people of Dolphin Bay will pay any heed to a stranger."

Cassie's shoulders slumped.

"I just thought we could help her out a bit. She's a nomad. She'll be gone in a few days."

"Alright," Anna said grudgingly. "We'll take her on. But ask me first next time."

The phone rang, interrupting them. Vicki Bauer was on the other side and she was hysterical.

"Calm down, Vicki," Anna commanded. "I can't make head or tail of what you are saying."

Cassie stood up and started clearing the table, listening to her mother's one sided conversation. She had finished loading the dishwasher by the time Anna hung up.

"Cody's in trouble," Anna declared.

"I gathered that much," Cassie said. "What happened, Mom?"

"The police just arrested Cody." Anna ignored Cassie's gasp and continued. "Apparently, he was going out of town with some friends. The police thought he was making a run for it. They brought him in."

"What was he doing?" Cassie asked.

"He was going south for some music festival. He insists he had no intention of fleeing town."

"That's kinda hard to believe, Mom. Surely the police warned him against leaving town? Every movie old or new has a scene where the sheriff tells the suspect not to skip town."

"What's done is done. We need to think about how to get him out now."

"I can call Teddy Fowler. He's the detective on the case."

"I think we should go there in person," Anna said. "That might make a difference."

"Where's your friend Vicki?"

"She's still at home, poor thing."

"We can pick her up on the way over," Cassie said. "Grab your purse, Mom."

Cassie's temperamental car refused to start after three tries.

"Let's just walk there," Anna said.

Cassie told her mother to be patient and tried again. The car obliged and Cassie set off with the usual screech of tires. They made a brief stop to get Vicki and pulled up in front of the police station fifteen minutes later.

"Where is he? Where's my son?" Vicki asked loudly as soon as they went in.

The clerk at the desk told them to sit down and be quiet. Cassie spotted Teddy Fowler and made a beeline for him.

"Hey Teddy!" she greeted him brightly.

Teddy was happy to see her.

"Cassie? What are you doing here?"

Cassie nodded toward Vicki and her mother.

"I'm with them. Did you really just arrest Cody Bauer?"

"We had no choice, Cassie. He was fleeing town."

"From what I heard, he was just heading to a music festival."

"That's what he says, of course. I'm not naïve enough to believe him."

"But he's innocent, Teddy. There are so many other suspects."

"Yeah? Like who? I'm sorry, Cassie. We were going to bring him in today anyway. He sealed his own fate by trying to escape."

Cassie went over to talk to Anna.

"Teddy won't budge."

"Do you know anyone who works here?" Anna asked Vicki. "Someone who can talk to the detective on your behalf?"

Vicki shook her head.

"Let me make a call," Anna said.

Cassie had a hunch about what her mother was up to. Anna came back a few minutes later and confirmed it.

"I talked to Gino. He wants to talk about this in person. He's waiting for us at Mystic Hill."

Cassie's car started at the first try this time. Vicki sat mutely in the back seat, dabbing her eyes with a tissue.

"You need to keep it together for Cody," Anna told her. "He's depending on you."

Gino was waiting outside in the portico when they reached the winery. He ushered them in.

Cassie looked on as Anna gave him a brief account of what

had happened.

"The police have some solid evidence against your son," Gino told Vicki. "I think they have plenty of ground to detain him today."

"But he's innocent," Vicki wailed. "I know my boy. He may be hot headed but he would never harm anyone, least of all, a girl he loved."

"I have been retired for a while," Gino said. "I don't have any control over what the police do. I can just try to learn what they are thinking."

"Teddy Fowler is handling Cody's case," Cassie told him.

Gino stepped away from the ladies and placed a call. He was on the phone for a while. He didn't look optimistic when he hung up.

"I am sorry. They are holding Cody for tonight. They will charge him tomorrow."

"What about all the other suspects?" Cassie asked. She whirled around and looked at Anna. "Tell him about the old guy, Mom."

"We think Briana was having an affair with her professor," Anna told Gino. "He might have wanted her out of the way."

"The evidence of the fingerprints is too strong," Gino explained. "I suggest you find out more about this professor. What was his relationship with Briana? Did he even have a motive to kill her?"

Chapter 26

Anna slept in late the next day. All the running around the previous night had wiped her out. She and Cassie had stayed with Vicki until she calmed down a bit. Anna herself had felt overwhelmed by the stressful situation.

Cassie sat in the kitchen, nursing a cup of coffee. She poured Anna a cup.

"I didn't realize how late it was," she said. "Why didn't you wake me up?"

"You needed the rest, Mom."

Cassie suggested they go to the diner for breakfast. Anna agreed reluctantly. They were ready to leave half an hour later. Cassie insisted Anna ride with her in the car.

"You never know. We might have to go somewhere later."

Anna had talked to Julie about the professor the previous night. Julie was going to tap her network of friends and try to get some information. Until Julie actually found something, it was a waiting game.

The town was buzzing with the news of Cody's arrest.

"About time the police did something," one righteous voice said.

Lara Crawford was sitting at a booth with a couple of women from her staff. She smiled maliciously when she saw Anna.

"Well, well, look who's decided to show her face. You are shameless, aren't you?"

"You leave my mother alone," Cassie roared. "We can sue you for harassment, you know."

"Honey, I am the mayor of this town. No judge is going to rule against me."

"Don't get cocky, Lara," Anna warned.

"On the contrary, you're the one who's strutting around when you should be locked up. You know what happened to your friend's son, don't you? You are next."

"Cody's innocent," Anna stressed, even though she wasn't so sure of it herself. "I'm going to prove it."

Cassie pulled Anna away from Lara's table and led her to a booth at the back. She ordered the breakfast special for both of them.

"I want to get out of here as soon as possible," Anna whispered. "But I'm ravenous."

"Take your time and enjoy your meal, Mom. You can't let that vile woman run you out of here."

Their food arrived quickly and the waitress didn't linger to gossip after Anna glared at her. Neither of them talked much as they focused on eating. Anna placed a twenty on the table and motioned Cassie to get up as soon as they were done.

The sky was overcast and a heavy wall of mist hung over the bay. Anna felt the whole atmosphere was rife with anticipation. A few magnolia blossoms lay on the sidewalk in front of the bookstore. Anna absentmindedly picked one up and breathed in its fragrance.

Cassie hesitated outside the door.

"Do you mind keeping me company today?" Anna asked her.

Cassie smiled eagerly and followed her inside.

Anna started dusting the shelves but her mind was preoccupied. She jumped when the phone rang. It was just a customer who wanted to know if they had the latest bestseller in stock.

"I wonder what's keeping her," Anna mumbled as she went into the pantry to make coffee.

"Why don't you call her, Mom?"

"She'll be here when she's ready."

The bell behind the door jingled just then and Julie obliged them by sweeping in.

"I called Mary. She should be here soon."

"Tell me what you found," Anna said anxiously. "We can fill Mary in later."

The door opened again and Mary arrived, looking a bit harried.

"What is it? What's happened?"

Julie flipped the sign on the door to 'Closed' and told everyone to settle down.

"You owe me big time, Anna."

Anna's impatience was written clearly on her face. Julie took notice and forged ahead.

"I made some calls. A lot of calls. The professor in question is Gordon Hunt. He's a senior professor in the English department. A bit whimsical but quite popular."

"Is he a short man who wears tweed suits all the time?" Anna asked. "I think I remember John talking about him."

"I don't know," Julie shrugged. "I have never come across him myself."

"Go on," Anna urged.

"Well, once I found out who he was, it was easier to find out more. One of my friends is in the local knitting club. Gordon's wife is in this club, apparently."

"Weren't you in the knitting club, Mary?" Anna asked.

"I stopped going a year ago. I haven't had the time since the latest grandchild."

"What did your friend say?" Cassie prompted, steering

them back on track.

"Gordon's wife is sure he's having an affair. She talked to my friend about it."

"His wife knew?" Anna asked incredulously. "She could have gone after Briana."

"The wife doesn't know who Gordon was having an affair with. My friend is sure about it."

"The wife could be lying," Cassie pointed out.

"That's right," Anna said. "Why would she advertize the fact that she knew her husband's mistress?"

"All valid points," Julie agreed. "But they don't fly here. The wife has an airtight alibi."

A collective groan filled the room.

"The knitting club meet at each other's homes one by one. They were at Gordon Hunt's house the day Briana died."

"What time was this meeting?" Anna asked urgently.

"They met around 3:30. Tea and snacks were served. They did whatever they do at these meetings. Then the wine started flowing. It's their usual jam, it seems. They get drunk on wine, order pizza or Chinese food and crib about their husbands."

"Was Gordon Hunt's wife present all the time?" Anna asked.

"My friend said she was. She said all the other ladies present will confirm it."

"So the wife's no use to us," Cassie said, her voice laden with disappointment.

"I'm not done yet," Julie said. "You know who was Not present in the house during the meeting? Gordon Hunt!"

"That's very typical," Mary said. "Men don't want to be around a flock of twittering women. And the women don't like to have a man underfoot."

"That's fine, Mary," Anna said. She looked at Julie. "I don't see how that helps us."

Julie gave a secretive smile.

"Gordon came in just as the group was breaking up. My friend said he looked disheveled. His clothes were muddy. There was a tear in his jacket and he was all fidgety."

"Did he have some kind of accident?" Cassie asked.

"That's what his wife thought. She wanted to take him to the hospital. Gordon waved her off. Said he was playing golf at the resort and had a small mishap. He slipped and fell in a pond. He had a slight sprain in his ankle but he was fine otherwise."

"What else did your friend say?" Anna asked.

"She didn't stick around after that," Julie told them.

The bell over the door dinged again.

"We are closed," Anna said automatically. Then her mouth hung open as she stared at the slight blue haired girl standing before her.

"It's okay, Mom," Cassie said. "This is Rain, the girl I told you about."

"What are you doing here, sweetie?" Mary asked kindly. "Did you want to talk to me?"

"I'm here to work," the girl spoke up. "This lady here offered me a job."

"There's not a lot to do here, I'm afraid," Anna said. "Why don't we take it one week at a time?"

"Okay," the girl said with a shrug.

"We need to clear something up first," Anna said grimly. "Mary told me about your little accident. Did you know Briana?"

"No Ma'am."

"Then what were you doing with her phone number?"

Rain looked at Mary but didn't say anything. Mary turned red as she tried to think of a response.

"I was cleaning," she said lamely. "There were a bunch of brochures lying around. I wanted to tidy them up."

"It's your house," Rain said with a shrug. She stared into Anna's eyes. "This girl, Briana, she promised to pay me something. But she never got back. I got her phone

216

number off the college website."

"See?" Mary gushed. "She had nothing to do with Briana."

Anna told Rain to come back the next day.

"What's next, Mom?" Cassie asked. "Shall we go talk to Teddy?"

"You don't have any proof against Gordon Hunt," Julie said. "What are you going to tell the police?"

"I'm going to talk to Gino about this," Anna said. "I think he will give us the right advice."

"Teddy might be more inclined to listen to him," Cassie added.

"Not unless he has something better to say," Julie argued. "If Gino had that kind of pull, Cody would never have been arrested."

Anna uttered a cry of exclamation.

"I have a hunch. Let's go to the diner first."

Anna refused to say any more about it. Cassie and the Firecrackers waited on the sidewalk while Anna locked the bookstore. They trooped after her as she walked purposefully toward the Yellow Tulip Diner.

Twenty minutes later, they were all piling into Julie's big SUV, headed for the Mystic Hill Winery.

Anna felt confused by all the new facts that had surfaced

that morning. She hoped Gino Mancini would help her make some sense out of it.

Chapter 27

"I am so sorry to bother you again," Anna told Gino as she scrambled out of the car. "This is becoming a habit."

"A habit you will keep up, I hope," Gino Mancini said suavely.

Anna blushed but she found herself drawn to Gino's dimples.

"Let's go in," Gino said, ushering everyone in. "It's past noon so I arranged a light lunch for you ladies. I am sure you can use some refreshment."

"That sounds lovely," Mary said.

Cassie and Julie gave their approval.

"We don't want to impose," Anna said, sounding embarrassed.

"Please … it was no trouble. My housekeeper rarely gets a chance to impress guests."

Gino waited until everyone had filled their plates from the tiny buffet. The ladies had a choice of smoked salmon and cheese on crackers, tiny cheese quesadillas with fresh guacamole and grilled chicken on skewers with a sweet chili sauce. There was a big bowl of fresh fruit salad to round everything up.

Anna tasted everything just to be polite. Gino noticed her anxiety and nodded at her.

"Tell me what you have been up to, Anna."

"We tracked down the man Briana was having an affair with. Now we need your help in convincing the police to bring him in."

"The police won't move without any actual proof."

Anna repeated everything they had learned about Gordon Hunt.

"He went to the diner with Briana. The girl at the diner recognized him."

"He wasn't breaking any laws though, was he?" Gino asked.

"I am sure it's against the rules to have an affair with your student," Anna said. "It's definitely not ethical. Gordon's wife is sure he was having an affair. And we can place him and Briana together in multiple places."

"But they were never seen arguing, were they?" Gino asked.

Anna felt helpless.

"Is there nothing you can do?" she asked Gino.

"Hold on a second, Mom," Cassie said, tapping some keys on her phone. "I called Sherrie when you were talking to that waitress at the diner. Sherrie had Briana's laptop. She found some old emails between Gordon and Briana."

"What do they say?" Anna cried.

"There are a lot of them. She says they start off as love letters and get more intense. Briana wanted Gordon to marry her."

Anna stared at Gino.

"Does that help?"

"You have convinced me, Anna," Gino sighed. "Let me talk to Teddy Fowler."

Gino went inside his den to make the call. The women noshed on the food while they waited for him to come back. Gino came back some time later.

"Teddy agreed to bring the professor in for questioning."

The ladies cheered and clapped their hands.

"Now what?" Anna asked.

"Now we wait," Gino said. "This could take a while."

Anna thanked him profusely. She hovered around him while he fixed a plate for himself.

"Why don't you invite Gino for dinner at our place, Mom?" Cassie asked, widening her eyes suggestively.

"Great idea," Anna said, turning red. "What do you like to eat, Gino?"

"I'm not picky," Gino said. "Surprise me!"

They chatted for a while until Gino put his plate down.

"I need to get back to the store," Anna said reluctantly. "I hope we get some good news soon."

"We are having a big potluck at the bookstore," Mary told Gino. "Everyone in town is invited. We are hoping to get some signatures in favor of Anna's café."

"Anna told me about the petition," Gino told her. "Count me in."

Julie drove them back to the bookstore. The group dispersed soon after that. Mary needed to go home and start getting dinner ready. Julie had to get back to her writing. Cassie wanted to talk to Bobby and take a nap.

Anna went about her daily chores, wondering what was happening at the police station.

Vicki Bauer burst into the store as the sky darkened, Cody in tow. Anna had just started to close up.

"You did it, Anna, you did it!" Vicki yelled. "How can I ever thank you?"

Cody stood by quietly, looking dazed. Anna pulled him into a hug.

"Thank you for believing in me, Mrs. Butler," he mumbled.

"Is it over?" Anna asked Vicki.

"We don't know much yet," Vicki replied. "I'm just happy they let him go."

"Go home and relax now. I think the worst is behind us."

Anna went home as soon as Vicki left with her son.

Cassie was watching Casablanca in the living room, a big tub of popcorn in her lap.

"How many times are you going to watch that movie?" Anna grumbled goodnaturedly.

"What's for dinner, Mom?" Cassie asked, ignoring her. "I know you hate salad so I didn't make anything."

"How about Chicken Piccata?" Anna asked. "Or Ravioli Lasagna?"

Cassie chose the lasagna.

Anna pulled out a big bag of her homemade cheese ravioli from the freezer along with a carton of her red sauce. Now she just needed to grate some cheese and assemble the casserole.

Cassie had made a salad and set the table by the time Anna came out of her shower. They had barely taken a bite of their dinner when the doorbell rang.

Anna opened the door to find Gino Mancini at the doorstep.

"Come in, come in," she said. "This is like déjà vu."

"Am I interrupting your dinner again?" Gino asked.

"Why don't you join us?" Anna asked. "It's just a simple

lasagna though. Very last minute."

Gino had come bearing news.

"Gordon confessed," he said. "He was a hard nut to crack though."

Anna and Cassie listened with their mouths hanging open as Gino narrated the sordid tale.

"At first, he denied any attachment to Briana. Then he admitted he hired her as a stand-in."

"Why did he need a date?" Anna asked. "He has a wife, doesn't he?"

"That part is not clear. Gordon was used to girl students fawning over him. He said it wasn't his fault Briana fell in love with him."

"What about all those times they met at the resort?" Anna asked. "He can't deny that, surely?"

"And what about the emails on Briana's laptop?" Cassie asked.

Gino took a big bite of his lasagna and nodded.

"He denied everything until the police presented the evidence to him one by one. They were testing his fingerprints while he was being questioned. Turns out his prints too were found on that bat."

Anna and Cassie both sucked in a breath.

"Briana dreamed of marrying him but Gordon had no intention of leaving his wife. Briana gave him an ultimatum. That's when he planned to kill her."

"He must have been thrilled when the police arrested Cody."

"That was his plan all along," Gino said. "Gordon talked Briana into borrowing the baseball bat, knowing it would have Cody's prints on it. Then he took Briana out to the diner and made sure Cody would see them there. He picked a fight with Cody so people would remember how Cody had lost his temper and got violent."

"I guess Briana played into his hands by calling the police on Cody," Anna mused.

"He couldn't have planned it better," Gino explained. "He made up some excuse and asked Briana to meet him in the redwood forest urgently. He knew she was supposed to meet Cody at that time."

"Poor Briana," Cassie sighed. "She never suspected him?"

"She fell for his charms. He has done this a lot, it seems. He has affairs with the young girls and dumps them when they try to get serious."

"That sounds unreal," Anna said. "None of the girls ever came forward?"

"He controlled their grades and their future. That's exactly how rascals like him get away."

"I hope they put him away for a long time," Cassie said.

"What about Cody?" Anna asked.

"Cody's free." Gino scraped his plate clean and took a second helping. "He could never have done it, you know. He doesn't have enough strength in his elbow to really swing a bat."

"His old elbow injury!" Anna exclaimed. "How did I miss that!"

"Everyone missed it, apparently," Gino said. "Teddy Fowler stumbled on it while he was interviewing Cody."

Gino stuck around for a while after dinner.

"The wine tasting event is coming up," he said when Anna saw him off at the door. "I hope you will come as my guest."

Anna grinned and nodded. "I am looking forward to it."

"Can I call him your boyfriend now, Mom?" Cassie asked with a wink as soon as Anna shut the door.

"It's your turn to do the dishes," Anna reminded her before heading to her room.

Epilogue

The party was in full swing. Bayside Books was overflowing with people enjoying a glass of wine, chatting with their friends and having a good time. A row of grills had been set up outside the store, facing the Coastal Walk and the bay. Mary's husband Ben and his buddy Rory Cunningham had volunteered to work them. Burgers and franks flamed on the grill and there was a lively discussion about whose technique was best.

Anna stood near the entrance, welcoming the steady stream of guests. Two long tables groaned with the weight of dishes overflowing with a variety of food. Julie had made her famous baked beans. Mary brought two kinds of pasta salad along with a pecan pie. There were five kinds of potato salad, roasted corn on the cob and fried chicken and biscuits.

Everyone had brought a dish and the potluck was a roaring success.

Gino Mancini had donated the wine for the event. Anna had protested at the extravagance but he hadn't taken no for an answer. Cassie had teased her mercilessly about it. Gino stood behind another table, pouring wine for the good people of Dolphin Bay. He was inviting everyone to the wine festival at Mystic Hill.

Cassie was in charge of the most important task of the day.

She stood behind a big hardcover notebook, urging people to sign the petition for Anna's café. She had dialed up the charm, raving about the delicious treats the town could expect from the café. A platter of Anna's delicious cupcakes stood next to the book, a reward for anyone who showed their support.

Julie and Mary mingled with the guests, making sure they each had a drink or a plate full of food. Most of the people knew each other well. A few tourists had also walked in, lured by the quaint small town event.

Cassie was talking to a couple of ladies she didn't recognize when she felt a frisson of excitement. Dylan Woods gave her a nod and picked up a pen to sign his name.

"Anna's looking good," he said. "It's nice to see her recovering so well."

Cassie felt her mind going blank.

"She's got spunk," she croaked. "I mean, yeah, thanks."

Dylan flashed a cheeky smile and took a big bite of his hot dog.

"Great party."

Cassie nodded mutely as he walked to the food table to fix himself a fresh plate.

Jose Garcia arrived, dressed in a Hawaiian shirt, grinning from ear to ear.

"I'm off to Cabo tomorrow," he beamed.

Anna's face fell.

"You promised to wait, Jose," she said under her breath.

"You will love the new owner," Jose winked. "I am sure you can work out a long term lease."

"Huh?" Anna was confused.

Julie walked over to them and glared at Jose.

"Have you let the cat out of the bag?"

"Not yet, but you better hurry. I came to say goodbye to everyone."

"What's going on, Julie?" Anna asked.

"Hold your breath," Julie said, her eyes shining. "I bought the store next door, Anna."

Anna almost screamed in surprise.

"But why? And how?"

Julie shrugged. "Let's just say I was looking to invest. I got a big advance for my next book."

Mary had heard them talking and walked over. She called her two friends in for a group hug.

"This is a day for surprises," Anna said, wiping her tears. "Agnes and her sister came in to sign the petition. She said she wasn't convinced I was innocent but the town could use a new café. She ate two cupcakes."

"We have enough signatures to sway the licensing board," Mary said. "You better get ready to bake, Anna."

Rain was going around the room, collecting trash and cleaning up where needed. Her hair was magenta now. Anna had reluctantly admitted she was happy with the extra help.

Vicki arrived with Cody in tow. A quiet murmur rippled through the room as people recognized Cody. Anna hugged them and Julie fixed them a plate. Things returned to normal.

A sudden hush fell over the room as a surprise guest arrived. No one had invited her. Lara Crawford stood at the door, her mouth set in a superior smirk.

"Live it up while you can, Anna."

"You need to leave, Lara," Anna said calmly. "You are not welcome here."

"I wanted to give you the news myself," Lara smiled. "The police have reopened John's case. You will be hearing from them soon."

Julie, Mary and Cassie had gathered around Anna.

"You can go now," Julie glared. "This is a private event."

Lara gave a malicious grin and spun around on her heel. She had accomplished her purpose.

Anna's face had clouded over. Cassie held her shaking hand in a tight grip and urged her to calm down.

Gino had joined the group.

"We are going to face this together, Anna. This is a slur on my reputation too."

Anna smiled her way through the next two hours. Finally, all the food had been eaten and the guests went home. Julie, Mary and Anna sat huddled in an alcove, sipping a celebratory glass of wine.

Rain and Cassie were dismantling the tables and putting the room back to order. Rain held a stack of utensils in her arms, barely able to see where she was going. Cassie backed into her with a jug of iced tea. The dishes fell to the ground with a clatter. Cassie's knee popped and she was about to go down too when Rain grabbed her and pulled her up. A wallet fell out of the girl's clothes and burst open on the floor.

Rain scrambled to pick up everything and stuff it back in the purse. Cassie picked up a laminated card that had fallen a few inches away from the other stuff.

"You missed this ..." she began saying.

Rain pulled at the card in Cassie's hand just when she began exclaiming over it.

"Is that your license picture? I take the most horrible license pictures."

Cassie won the tussle and brought the card closer to her face, eager to stare at the picture. Her smile froze on her face, her excitement changing into shock and horror in the fraction of a second.

The card slipped from her hand and fell to the ground.

The Firecrackers had come over to help the girls up.

"Cassie?" Anna asked sharply. "You turned white as a sheet. What's the matter?"

Mary picked up the piece of plastic and started reading what was written on it.

"Meg Butler!" she exclaimed.

She stared in disbelief at the slight girl with the shock of magenta hair. The girl stared back.

"But you said your name is Rain," Mary said hoarsely.

Rain shrugged but said nothing.

"Is it true?" Anna asked, her face a kaleidoscope of emotions. "Don't be afraid, sweetie."

Rain nodded once.

The tears began streaming down Anna's face.

"I have been looking for you."

***

Thank you for reading this book. If you enjoyed this book, please consider leaving a brief review. Even a few words or a line or two will do.

As an indie author, I rely on reviews to spread the word about my book. Your assistance will be very helpful and greatly appreciated.

I would also really appreciate it if you tell your friends and family about the book. Word of mouth is an author's best friend, and it will be of immense help to me.

Many Thanks!

Author Leena Clover

http://leenaclover.com

Leenaclover@gmail.com

http://twitter.com/leenaclover

https://www.facebook.com/leenaclovercozymysteryb ooks

Other books by Leena Clover

Pelican Cove Cozy Mystery Series

Cupcakes and Celebrities

Berries and Birthdays

Sprinkles and Skeletons

Waffles and Weekends

Muffins and Mobsters

Parfaits and Paramours

Truffles and Troubadours

Sundaes and Sinners

Meera Patel Cozy Mystery Series

Gone with the Wings

A Pocket Full of Pie

For a Few Dumplings More

Back to the Fajitas

Christmas with the Franks

Acknowledgements

Launching a new series is not easy. The world of Dolphin Bay came alive after sounding off ideas with my closest confidantes. The women in my family provided the inspiration for the Butlers, allowing me to create a series about strong, fearless heroines who fight against the odds.

A big thank you to my family and friends for standing by me. Their unwavering support keeps me going every day.

I am grateful for all the beta readers and reviewers who take the time to read and evaluate my work and provide early feedback. They help me improve with every book.

I am also thankful to all the readers who give my books a chance. I hope you keep those emails and messages coming for they surely brighten my day.

Join my Newsletter

Get access to exclusive bonus content, sneak peeks, giveaways and much more. Also get a chance to join my exclusive ARC group, the people who get first dibs on all my new books.

Sign up at the following link and join the fun.

Click here →
http://www.subscribepage.com/leenaclovernl

I love to hear from my readers, so please feel free to connect with me at any of the following places.

Website – http://leenaclover.com

Twitter – https://twitter.com/leenaclover

Facebook –
http://facebook.com/leenaclovercozymysterybooks

Email – leenaclover@gmail.com